CHEERLEADERS®

#14

LIVING IT UP

JENNIFER SARASIN

SCHOLASTIC INC.
New York Toronto London Auckland Sydney

ISBN 0-590-33930-3

12 11 10 9 8 7 6 5 4 3 2   6 7 8 9/8 0 1/9

Printed in the U.S.A.   01

CHEERLEADERS

LIVING IT UP

CHEERLEADERS

CHAPTER

1

The Pineland Mall had been getting more crowded lately, so the city fathers had decided to destroy the little pocket park next to the mall so they could put in an additional parking lot. The six cheerleaders couldn't have been more disgusted.

Yet, they were drawn to the place. As soon as the heavy equipment moved in and started digging up trees, the cheerleaders couldn't stop themselves from watching the destruction. They generally spent a lot of their time at the mall — when practice was over for the day, when Saturdays were long and dull, or when they just felt like hanging out. Now, they felt they had to be there, until the last tree was dug up and the cement started pouring in. Awful as it was, they felt compelled to see it with their own eyes.

Pres Tilford was feeling pretty depressed these days, anyway. The destruction of the park just compounded the rotten mood he'd been in ever since Claudia Randall had gone to California. Claudia, whom he loved the way he'd never thought he'd be capable of loving. Claudia of the long legs and violet eyes, and that soft southern accent that drove him wild. If only she'd been straight with him from the beginning and told him what was wrong with her. But she hadn't wanted him to know. She couldn't have stood his pity, she said, and that's why she'd kept quiet about her condition.

She was a champion horsewoman, but had fallen off her horse. A bone fragment in her back had dislodged. It had been pressing against her spinal column ever since, and if it wasn't operated on soon, she might eventually be paralyzed. Since Claudia had gone to California for the operation that would either fix her spine, leave her paralyzed, or kill her, Pres had been hurting badly. If only he'd known sooner about the terrible secret she'd kept from him and from everyone. Now that he knew how much he could care for another human being, he just hoped it wasn't too late for him.

He was always thinking about her, even when he was cheering or doing his homework or driving his Porsche. Every once in a while, even sitting in the mall with the group, he'd look up to see someone passing by and think it was Claudia. Of course, that was impossible — she was miles away — but it didn't make any difference. When his friends saw that distant look in his eyes, they would invariably try to snap him out of it. Which was what Walt Manners was trying to do right now.

"I don't see why they have to destroy everything beautiful in the name of progress, do you, Pres?" Walt asked.

Pres came back to reality in a flash. The only way he knew to drag himself out of his blues was to joke, even when he didn't think anything was funny. "Well," he said, "if you don't have anywhere to park your Jeep, you can come here. Ipso facto — the new parking lot is a vital necessity of your life."

"Oh, Pres, you're so practical!" Mary Ellen Kirkwood scoffed. "Where's the poet in your soul?"

Pres began examining himself in a panic, searching for the lost poet.

"Probably never had one to begin with," Angie Poletti said. "The care and feeding of Pres's Porsche is emphatically more important to him."

"Now, just a second," Pres protested, but the others were laughing so hard, it was difficult for him to make too much of a fuss. Pres's Porsche was testimony to the fact that the Tilfords could buy and sell most anything and anyone in town. The fact that Pres argued with his father nonstop and disapproved of his parents' standards did not detract from his love of expensive things.

"I don't know. Do we really need more parking?" Olivia Evans asked philosophically as she leaned comfortably on Walt's shoulder. The two of them had been an item for a long time now, and their relationship had withstood just about every test. "More parking means more customers, which means more conspicuous consumption. Wouldn't

3

we all be happier just camping out in the woods, listening to the chirping of the birds and the scurry of squirrels?"

Her friends looked at her in utter disbelief, and then Walt pushed her off the bench. She landed on the ground, laughing hysterically, delighted to have succeeded in putting them on.

"No, but to get back to the main point here," Nancy Goldstein said, "the whole town is just becoming too commercial. When we moved here last year, it was because my folks felt small town life would be good for us. And now Tarenton is getting just as big as Cedar Grove or Garrison or Wickfield." Nancy had felt so much the outsider when she first started at Tarenton High, and it wasn't just because she was one of the few Jewish kids in school. It had been such a change for her, living in a place where almost everybody knew you by name. Now, of course, she was part of the Varsity Cheerleading Squad, dating Ben Adamson, the star center on the Tarenton basketball team. She was very much one of the in-crowd. Still, that didn't stop the feeling that she was sometimes a stranger in a strange land.

"Let's take a walk," Walt suggested. "We've been sitting around here for an hour. I can't watch that bulldozer dig up another tree."

They got up, reluctantly glancing back once more at the machine whose gaping orange metal jaws were biting down on the earth, uprooting everything in their wake. Mary Ellen shuddered, then hurried on in front of the group, leading them on to Marnie's, the most fashionable boutique in the mall. There was something she very much wanted to see over there.

"Hey, isn't that you?" Pres demanded, as they approached the store. A large video screen had been set up to the right of the entrance, and a tape was playing on it. A succession of models on camera were marching down a runway, displaying the new spring fashions.

"Sure is," Mary Ellen grinned. "How do you like me on film?"

He squinted at the screen, then back at her. "Well, aside from that weird harem outfit you have on, you don't look bad. When did this all come about?"

"Mrs. Gunderson decided we could rope in a lot more business with these ads," Mary Ellen explained. Mrs. Gunderson, who owned Marnie's, had been a model in New York for years and knew how to sell clothes.

"But see, this is just what I was talking about!" Olivia exclaimed. She looked down at her well-worn jeans and bottle-green turtleneck and did a small pirouette. "I have all the wardrobe I need. Why does some stupid commercial have to convince me that I'm poorly dressed?" Olivia was the youngest of the group, a tiny ball of energy. After a hard, sickly childhood spent in and out of hospitals, after operations to correct a heart problem, Olivia had bounced back with a vengeance. Now, she was as healthy as they came and determined to stay that way.

"Hey," Mary Ellen grinned. "I don't think the videos are a bad idea at all." More than anything in the world, Mary Ellen dreamed of going to

New York to become a model. With her exquisite face, blonde hair that curled to her shoulders, and a figure most girls would kill for, she had a pretty good chance. She certainly had the ambition to push her way to the top.

But one thing stopped her, and that was Patrick Henley. Patrick was the school photographer, which meant that he would have had to be around Mary Ellen a lot even if he weren't in love with her. But he was also his father's son, and his father owned Henley Trash, a private garbage collection business. Patrick had his own truck and helped his father on his daily route. For Mary Ellen to relegate herself to a life in a small town as a garbage collector's wife was too horrible a thought to contemplate. And yet, since Patrick was funny, kind, sexy, and devastatingly wonderful, she couldn't really rule out the possibility. She was terribly confused about Patrick — their goals were always colliding, like meteors in space.

"Who cares about videos?" Pres demanded. "The really crucial thing is, are we going to win against Northfield next Saturday, or what?"

"Of course we are," Nancy nodded. "With Ben playing, how can we lose?"

The others began talking about the upcoming game, but Walt stood aside, watching something at the other side of the mall.

"C'mon, Walt," Olivia said, tugging on his arm. "We're going for pizza."

"Who *is* that guy?" Walt demanded, pointing across the way. "I keep seeing him around town, popping up around corners, talking to the kids."

They followed Walt's gaze and saw what he

saw: a thin, anxious-looking man in his late thirties, wearing an oversized corduroy jacket and a long wool scarf around his neck. He had his dark glasses propped on top of his head and was talking to a group of kids who were gathered around him.

"You know, now that you mention it," Pres said thoughtfully, "he *does* look kind of familiar. I saw him in Cedar Grove last week, talking to some kids on the street. And I think he was at the mall last weekend, too."

"I saw him at school the other day, talking to Vanessa and her father," Nancy stated.

"Oh, a creep, huh?" Walt said emphatically. "We all know that any friend of Vanessa's has got to be nasty, conniving, and manipulative."

The others smiled their own personal agreements. Vanessa Barlow, daughter of the superintendent of schools, Dr. Barlow, was certainly their least favorite person in all of Tarenton. She had, at one time or another, arranged a variety of plots to make every one of them miserable. Her own greediness and anger at not having been picked for the Varsity Cheerleading Squad made her behave even worse to the six chosen ones than to anyone else at school.

"So you think this old guy is Van's new catch, do you?" Pres asked appraisingly. "Boy, he looks ancient." The man was now reaching into his jacket pocket. He came out with a bunch of cards and handed one to each kid in the circle around him.

"Oh, he's much too old for her," Angie protested. "Anyway, she wouldn't be hanging out

7

with him in front of her father, if she had any intention of dating him."

"A new teacher for Tarenton High?" Nancy guessed.

"I don't think so." Olivia stared at the guy intently. "He looks . . . well . . . different somehow. Not like a teacher."

"I've got it!" Mary Ellen declared with a snap of her fingers. "I bet he's a truant officer. Dr. Barlow must have hired him to take care of all the cutting that's been going on. And Vanessa probably decided to cozy up to him — trying to butter him up for the day he catches her out of school."

"Melon," Pres said, using Mary Ellen's hated nickname, "they don't even use truant officers in Tarenton anymore. And if they did, who ever heard of a truant officer who wears shades and high tops?"

She considered that one a minute. "A new trend in education?" she ventured. Pres gave her a look. "Well," she smiled sweetly, "try disappearing for chemistry tomorrow and see if you run into him."

The kids — all but Angie, who could eat any time and any place — had lost all their interest in pizza. They were more interested in the stranger, and in what he might be doing around town. So when he left the mall, they did, too. They piled into Walt's Jeep and began following him, like private detectives on a case. The problem was, he wasn't giving them a whole lot of clues. That afternoon, he visited the bike store, the beauty parlor, and the laundromat. Each place

8

he stopped, he glommed onto a group of kids and started talking. It was truly peculiar.

"The guy has to be a psycho. Maybe a child molester," Walt deduced. He liked to think of himself as a very savvy sleuth, and was always concocting impossible scenarios based on his own fantastic fantasies. But Sherlock Holmes he was definitely *not*.

"What makes you think that?" Olivia grinned. They were standing at the far corner of the laundromat, and their conversation was punctuated by the slosh and whirr of the washing machines. The stranger, over at the dryers with some of the kids from the Tarenton swim team, didn't seem to be aware of them.

"He's always following kids around. It's very suspicious," Walt nodded wisely.

"Tell you what, pal," Pres said. "You go up and ask the guy what he's doing around here. Always use the direct approach with criminals. It catches them off-guard."

"Are you kidding?" Walt gasped in mock horror. "I'd be a marked man. The next to go." He shuddered, then, taking Olivia by the arm, he led her to the door of the laundromat. "No, the only thing to do is avoid him at all costs. Maybe he'll go away."

Laughing, the six cheerleaders started down the street to the Jeep. They didn't see the man poke his head out the laundromat door and stare after them.

CHAPTER

Mary Ellen walked down the long basement corridor of Tarenton High, tying her lustrous blonde hair back with a crimson ribbon. She had finished dressing before the rest of the squad, and wanted just a few minutes to herself before the game started.

Some nights, the cheering seemed more important to her than others — and tonight was one of those times. There was something in the air, a certain feeling that everything she did, every move she made, was crucial. It was superstition, of course, but she could almost believe that the outcome of her whole life depended on the height of an eagle jump, the angle of an uplifted leg. If she did it just right, if she pleased the crowd just so much, then . . . well, anything could happen. If she messed up, her life would go on as usual, in its same old routine way.

Her cheerleader uniform was always sparkling clean and perfectly ironed right before a game. The short red skirt that opened when she jumped and leaped through the air to reveal sharp white pleats and the white sweater with its red "T" proudly emblazoned on it were just about her favorite clothes. She hated the fact that there was nothing else in her wardrobe that she really loved wearing, but those were the breaks of being poor.

Her father drove a bus and her mother was a bookkeeper; she could never blame them for not trying hard enough. She and her younger sister Gemma didn't lack for anything, exactly. It was just that there was so much she wanted out of life that they couldn't give her.

"There you are. *Wow*, if you don't mind my saying so." Patrick Henley was leaning casually against the closed door of the boiler room, focusing on her with his camera as she walked toward him. His shock of dark hair flopped easily over his forehead, and even with the camera in front of his face, she could tell he was smiling one of his lazy, sexy, incredible smiles.

"Patrick, you see me dressed like this constantly!" She shrugged, enormously pleased with the attention but not wanting to show it.

"For me, each time is the first time," he sighed, lowering the Pentax and slinging its strap over his shoulder. He came toward her then, his hands reaching for her.

"Don't you think we better get moving? The game's going to start any second." Mary Ellen

11

was anxious when she was alone with him, but she was lonely when he wasn't around. There was this awful split inside her, and she had no idea how to resolve it. "Patrick, not here," she begged as his large, muscular arms crept around her waist and drew her close.

"You don't mean that." He spoke to the soft golden hairs at the side of her neck, nuzzling her close, crushing the flowing curls with his free hand and letting his lips work their magic on her as they always did.

"Mary Ellen, are you down there?" The sound of another voice made them both self-conscious, and they drew apart reluctantly. "The squad is ready to go, but they can't find their captain, for heaven's sake!" Ardith Engborg, the cheer-leader's coach, was a small woman who commanded a great amount of respect, and when she was walking down the hall looking for you, you immediately jumped to attention.

"Coming, Mrs. Engborg," Mary Ellen said contritely, glancing longingly at the boy who stood there beside her, not touching her, looking innocent. "I was just letting Patrick in on some of the moves we have planned for halftime, so he'd be sure and get some good shots for the yearbook."

"Right." Ardith was no dummy; she knew what the captain of her cheerleaders felt about most things, and most people — particularly Patrick Henley.

"I want lots of spirit out there tonight, and lots of action," she stated. "Be sure to save the triple

Around the World for the final cheer if we're winning, but use it before halftime if we're losing. And don't let Pres get sloppy. He's been bothering me lately." She shook her head, nodding briskly to Patrick before marching away past them, toward the stairs that led up to the gym.

"Shall we?" Mary Ellen smiled and started after her, but she stopped dead in her tracks as a horrible sound pierced the air right beside her. It was halfway between a moan and a roar: the sound of a dinosaur waking from a millenium-long nap, or a monster rising up out of a misty swamp. "What is *that?*"

Patrick tapped the door beside them. "Boiler. That thing's been on its last legs so long, it can't even crawl. Even the screws that hold it together are old. I heard Pete the janitor saying he didn't think it could make it through another Tarenton winter."

Mary Ellen shook her head as the thing groaned again. "Poor old machine. Let's hope it'll get us through basketball season, at least."

They heard the crowd chanting even as they hit the top of the stairs, and there was hardly time for a quick kiss outside the gym before Mary Ellen was swept up by her squad and away from Patrick. She was physically propelled into the thick of the action, and her spirits lifted as she became aware of the excitement in the air. The bleachers were packed, the kids and parents standing up and demanding that the game begin. Mary Ellen cartwheeled her way to the center of the court, and the squad followed after her.

"Race along, run along,
Get that team where they live!
Move along, never wrong,
Tarenton's got
A lot to give!
Higher, HIGHER, *HIGHER*!
Yay, TEAM!"

They were sparkling tonight. Everyone agreed
afterwards that they were performing at the peak
of their abilities, which, on ordinary nights, were
considerable. Mary Ellen's smile could light up
the gym; Olivia's tumbling and gymnastic feats
forced a gasp from everyone in the bleachers.
Pres and Walt seemed to lift the girls effortlessly,
and their cartwheels and somersaults were perfectly in sync. As for Angie and Nancy, they
made a stunning pair as they worked together
through the first half of the game, alternately
giving their all to the cheers and encouraging the
pompon girls on the sidelines to work the crowd
until it dropped from yelling.

Ben Adamson, Nancy's boyfriend, tipped off
with the captain of the Northfield team and suddenly, he was all over the place. Ben, six-foot-
three and darkly handsome, was a person who
called a challenge to life — not just on the basketball court, but wherever he went. Sometimes,
watching him running the ball down the floor,
evading the opposition, dunking one basket after
another, Nancy wondered how long she was going
to be able to keep up with him. She'd dated him
even before he came to Tarenton, when he was the
star of the Garrison team, and had hated herself

for her disloyalty. Now that it was perfectly okay for her to go out with him, she occasionally felt overwhelmed by him. He was the kind of person you couldn't get too close to because he might just run you over.

Walt was in the process of lifting Nancy into the air when she felt him hesitate for a moment. Then, without missing a beat, he grabbed both her hands and swung her under his legs.

"What's the matter?" she hissed. Talking during a game was something Ardith really frowned on, but he looked so preoccupied, Nancy felt she had to ask.

"That guy. He's up there in the stands. Look — right next to Mrs. Oetjen." It was actually unusual to see both the principal and the superintendent of schools at the same game. Dr. Barlow and Mrs. Oetjen generally traded off. And yet tonight, they were both there. Vanessa Barlow was sitting beside her father, who was next to the stranger.

"I told you he was a truant officer," Mary Ellen said smugly, linking hands with Angie and Olivia for the flip over their braced arms.

"Well, at least he looks like he's enjoying the game," Olivia said, holding on for dear life as her captain took a breath and performed a flawless back flip that ended in a split.

"Why are you all so excited about this person?" Angie asked as they ran back to the sidelines, acknowledging the crowd's cheers. Now, right before halftime, Tarenton was winning easily, and when one of the Northfield guards fouled Ben, he took the ball into his huge hands and got his two free throws. The ball looped around and dropped into the basket the first time, and then the second, just before halftime.

The team ran out of the gym, followed by the cheerleaders, who were grinning with excitement. It was one thing to work well together throughout a hopeless game, where whatever you did couldn't affect the score or the spectators one way or another. But it was quite something else to be on top of the world, winning in every sense of the word. You were good, the players were good, and together you were making the evening a true Tarenton event.

"Did you see that guy?" Pres wiped his face and neck with a thin towel, and plopped himself down on the floor of the practice room.

"Sure," Angie shrugged. "But what's the big deal about him, anyway? Why don't you forget about him?"

"He just doesn't seem to belong here, that's all," Mary Ellen commented, easing herself to the floor in a backbend.

"Well, whatever he's here for, he's getting the best of it tonight. Boy, I wish we could do this well at every game," Walt said, his round earnest face moist with perspiration.

"Oh, there they are!" The sound of the principal's voice interrupted them. They were all frozen in place like gladiators who had just heard that the lions were waiting for them upstairs.

"Hi, Mrs. Oetjen." Mary Ellen nodded politely. She kept her voice level, but she was clearly surprised at the sight of the person Mrs. Oetjen had in tow. It was the stranger — dark glasses and

16

all. Behind him were Dr. Barlow and Vanessa.

"What do you say, kids?" The man had a low, nasal voice and a weird accent that none of the cheerleaders could place.

"Mr. Scheckner, I'd like to present our Tarenton cheerleaders. And boys and girls, this is Mr. Harris Scheckner, who's visiting us from New York City. He's very pleased with your performance. Of course," she added curtly, "we all are."

"You were really excellent tonight, *boys and girls,*" Vanessa said, making the principal's words sound terribly patronizing. Vanessa's lip curled whenever she was mad about something, and tonight, she looked terribly upset. The bitterness in her exotic, long-lashed stare was apparent, and her cheeks were flushed with the effort of smiling. She hated the six cheerleaders with a passion. "Harris," she said, casually putting a hand on the stranger's arm as if to claim him as her own personal find, "weren't they good?"

"Super. I mean, I have rarely been so — "

Mr. Scheckner was rudely interrupted at this point by the strange noise Mary Ellen and Patrick had heard earlier. Now the boiler sounded like it was definitely sick to its stomach.

"We've got to get that boiler fixed, Mrs. Oetjen," the superintendent of schools said anxiously. "It sounds dangerous."

"Oh, don't worry about it, sir," Walt grinned. "Just let it die a natural death and it'll be much happier."

"You were saying, Mr. Scheckner?" Mrs. Oetjen cleared her throat, trying to cover up for the faulty machinery in her school.

17

"Yeah, well, look, kids. I happen to be a director, see. I direct commercials for an ad agency in New York, and our client is looking for. . . ." He paused and whipped his glasses off dramatically. "He is looking for *you*. Doesn't know it yet, but I'm convinced. *You* are it. *You* are big. Let me explain it this way. . . ." He stretched his arms out and up, encompassing the world as he knew it. "All of America is waiting for the New Teenager, okay. Maybe I should say, the new embodiment of the old teenager, the one everybody used to love. The one who doesn't mug you on the street. The one who takes out the garbage every night, feeds the dog, and dries the dishes after dinner. So what I mean is, actually, our client is looking for an image. He wants *clean* to match his product, Clean Soap. And you are it."

The cheerleaders listened intently, trying not to let the expressions on their faces change as Harris Scheckner droned on. He sounded slightly demented.

"The upshot of this is, see, that we are filming a major production number-type shot for Clean Soap, and we need a group of kids who can move and yell and exude the kind of enthusiasm you had out there tonight. How about it?"

"You mean," Pres said slowly, "you want us to be in a commercial?"

"No, dear," Vanessa said sarcastically. "He wants you to take out the garbage and feed the dog." Her envy was showing, and that was not a pretty sight. Vanessa had always had a way of getting to Pres. Even when they weren't dating — and they hadn't done that in a long time, despite

Vanessa's efforts to fan the flame again — she knew how to press all the right buttons. Or the wrong ones, depending on her mood.

"I think you kids have the good looks, the talent, the oomph to be stars. You've got just the right mix of freshness and professionalism. I mean, we're not just talking one commercial here," Harris said importantly. "It's more like a showcase for what can come. I'm talking endorsements, I'm talking marketing, I'm talking exposure. Maybe a shot at a movie, who knows?"

The superintendent of schools cleared his throat as the warning buzzer sounded for the beginning of the second half of the game. "You kids have to get back up there right now, so we'll discuss this later. But Mr. Scheckner did want Mrs. Oetjen and me to know that he's been canvassing a lot of schools in this area lately and he's seen a lot of dance groups and cheering squads. You happen to be the finest, in his opinion. Now whether it goes any further or not depends on a number of things, right, Mrs. Oetjen?"

"That's right. Now, let's get back up there and win that game, shall we?" She took Mr. Scheckner by the arm and started to escort him to the stairs. But he turned back once, scanning the group through his poised fingers as though he were framing them before a camera lens. "See, kids, our idea here is to show the world that squeaky clean is more than just a phrase — it's a concept. Talk to you later." He raised his hand in a quick farewell, and then Mrs. Oetjen and Dr. Barlow dragged him away.

Vanessa slowly began to walk after her father, but she turned back once to smile tightly at the six stunned cheerleaders. "Don't count your chickens, folks. They haven't hatched yet. And remember, *I* met him first."

As she walked casually back toward the staircase, a very annoyed Ardith Engborg appeared around the corner, the air fairly crackling around her. "What's going on? We have a game going on upstairs, or didn't you notice? What's holding you up?"

The squad all started talking at once, but they couldn't get one coherent sentence out among them. Ardith caught only key words like *commercial, New York,* and *famous.* She raised her hands to her ears to block out the noise. "Come on, will you? We'll discuss this some other time. I don't understand a thing you're saying."

In a second, they couldn't be heard anyway. The crowds were cheering for Tarenton, which meant that the cheerleaders had a job to finish.

CHAPTER

The doorbell rang just as Nancy was putting the sliced turkey, ham, cole slaw, and potato salad on big platters. It was the cheerleaders' winter picnic special, an event that occurred frequently among them. This particular Monday afternoon, of course, they were getting together to discuss the Big News. Nancy's house was the logical place to meet and talk, since Mrs. Goldstein invariably allowed her daughter to entertain friends without weeks of preparation. As long as Nancy took care of the cooking and clean-up, she was free to invite people over at a moment's notice.

"Who's early?" Nancy grumbled, taking the stairs two at a time from the den in the basement. She arrived at the front door, panting, and pulled it open.

"Hi, sweetie!" Ben Adamson was leaning casually against the doorframe, looking devastating in his sheepskin jacket and biker's cap pulled down over his dark hair. He swooped her up in his arms and spun her around.

"Hey, put me down!" Nancy said, laughing.

"Anybody here yet?" Ben asked, reluctantly doing as she requested and following her inside. The instant the door was closed, he backed her up against it, pressing his lips firmly to hers. "I've missed you," he whispered when he let her come up for air again.

She grinned, touching his face as if to memorize it. "You just saw me Saturday night."

"Not enough. Never can see enough of you," he countered. This time, as he bent low, he gently wrapped his arms around her, savoring her sweet smell, the fall of her silky hair, the wonderful combination of ingredients that made up the girl he was so crazy about. He kissed her lightly, just brushing his mouth over hers, but as she wrapped her arms around his neck, the kiss became deeper, more urgent. The two of them would have stood there all day, locked together, if the doorbell hadn't rung. They both jumped a foot.

"Tell them to go away," Ben pleaded, reaching for her again.

"I can't. I invited them."

"Don't answer. Maybe they'll think you went out." His hands were at the back of her neck, making her yearn to give in.

"They'd wait," Nancy told him with a sigh. "They always do. Come on — we'll have time later," she promised as the doorbell rang again.

"Oh, okay. But I don't like it," Ben said

grouchily, moving aside so that she had access to the doorknob. "Not one bit."

"Hi, guys!" she said cheerfully, pulling the door ajar once again.

"Where've you been?" Walt asked, walking past Ben with a nod. "We've been standing here in the cold for an hour."

Nancy gave Ben a look. "Didn't hear you ring. I guess we must have been in the back . . . or something."

"Right. Or something," Pres said with a knowing look.

"Let's get busy and start eating. I'm famished." Angie made a beeline for the basement door, her highly tuned instincts telling her that a meal was imminent.

"How can you be hungry now?" Mary Ellen demanded. "How can you even think of food when Harris Scheckner is offering us the chance of a lifetime?" She did a little skip on her way toward the basement.

"He's from New York City," Walt reported to Ben excitedly as they all tromped downstairs. "In the advertising business."

"Yeah, and if you believe that, you're dumber than I thought." Ben was feeling left out already. Nancy had told him about the commercial and the trip to New York, and he wasn't really thrilled about the idea of his girl friend going off and having a wonderful time without him.

"No, look at his card." Walt grabbed it from his pocket. "It clearly says, *Harris Scheckner, Director of Media, HPS Advertising*." Walt set the cream-colored card with its high-tech black lettering on the table. "With an address and phone number and everything."

"Remember that so-called photographer who was going to make Angie into the hottest thing since Cheryl Tiegs?" Patrick asked. He was sitting on the floor, across the room from Mary Ellen. She had purposely moved away from him because she wanted to sit beside him so badly, and he could tell by the look on her face that the distance had nothing to do with her real feelings. "You've got to watch out for guys like that," he said.

Angie shut her eyes in a grimace, remembering how much trouble she could have gotten herself into if Mary Ellen, Nancy, and Olivia hadn't rushed in to save her in the nick of time.

"Yeah, right. There are all sorts of creeps and weirdos trying to sell something," Pres agreed, stalking the room like a nervous tiger in his cage. He had expected to hear from Claudia over the weekend, but she still hadn't called. He was getting worried.

"I don't see why you're all so down on this guy." Nancy shrugged. "I listened to him, you listened to him. How could Mrs. Oetjen and Dr. Barlow introduce us to somebody who wasn't on the up-and-up? It's perfectly straightforward," she continued. "He's looking for just the right types and that's what we are."

"It's wonderful to see Vanessa looking so green," Mary Ellen nodded, taking a bite of her sandwich. "The very thought that we might do something this exciting and she'd have to stay home in dull little Tarenton must make her brain tie itself into knots."

"I don't know. I think Vanessa would be great in commercials." Walt nodded. "For cockroach motels. 'Our guests check in, but they don't check out,' " he quoted, in an approximation of Vanessa's sultry sneer.

"You guys are fooling yourselves if you think this is going to be easy. Fame and fortune don't just fall in people's laps," Ben said, shaking a mayonnaise-smeared finger at the group.

"Why not?" Olivia demanded, scrambling to her feet and beginning to pace the room. "Why shouldn't we hit the big time in New York?" She grinned widely, then went over to sit beside Walt, who was busy picking the pimentos out of his cole slaw. "I think it sounds fabulous!"

"Well, let's check on the guy, at least," Patrick said determinedly, going to the telephone with the business card. "Mary Ellen tried this with that creep who was after Angie, and it worked. Okay, here goes. Area code two one two. . . ."

"What are you doing?" Pres asked, a funny smile on his face. As anxious as he was about Claudia, he was still able to get into the idea of living it up in New York.

"Are you really going to call them?" Nancy covered her face with her hands. "I can't look. He's really doing it!"

"Ah, good afternoon." Patrick tried hard to sound older than his years. "Is Mr. Scheckner in?"

There was a pause, where evidently the receptionist told him that Mr. Scheckner was out of town on a business trip.

"I see," Patrick responded. "Is there someone else in charge of commercial production I might speak with? Ah, who am I?" He looked at his friends, who were all sitting on the edges of their seats. They all shrugged. After all, he'd gotten himself into this mess — he could get himself out of it.

"I'm Patrick Henley," he said at last. "I'm a staff photographer with Kirkwood Associates."

Mary Ellen giggled; Pres looked at the ceiling in disbelief.

"Yes, ah, good afternoon," Patrick said when the receptionist had connected him. "I was talking with Harris Scheckner last week and he mentioned looking for a team of cheerleaders for that soap spot you folks are doing. Ah, can you tell me, has he found them yet? Kirkwood Associates wanted to get some preliminary stills of these kids."

Walt had a forkful of cole slaw poised at his lips; Olivia and Angie were standing beside Patrick, trying to listen to what was going on on the other end of the line. Nancy and Ben had their arms around each other, and Pres was pacing the floor. Mary Ellen just stood still, biting her nails.

"Oh, great. I see. Well, listen, tell Harris I'm sorry I missed him," Patrick said. "Hope we can all take a meeting sometime when I'm in the Big Apple. Right. Thanks. Bye." He hung up, his mouth twitching into a smile. Then he looked at the assembled group and burst out laughing.

"Well? For heaven's sake, don't keep us in suspense." Mary Ellen came over and began pounding Patrick on the shoulder.

"He's for real." Patrick grinned.

"Hey, man, *you* were real," Ben said, coming over to shake Patrick's hand. "A move like that takes guts, man."

"The guy told me Harris Scheckner just stumbled on the perfect bunch. 'A team of hicks from a tiny town called Tarenton.'"

"What?" Nancy was indignant.

"How dare he!" Angie grumbled.

"Listen, that's what *he* called you," Patrick shrugged. "Don't blame me."

"So, I guess our next step is planning when we're going to New York." Walt grinned, reaching for the last slice of turkey. Angie beat him to it, swiping it off the plate. When she was really happy about something, Angie couldn't stop herself — her appetite always got the better of her.

"Has anybody consulted parents about this?" Olivia asked with a frown. Her mother was a log-jam in her life. Every time there was something Olivia really wanted to do, Mrs. Evans claimed it was too difficult, too tiring, and too dangerous for her baby. These days, though, Livvy stood up to her mother and generally got her way, but it was tough.

"Forget parents. What about school? What about the powers that be? Mrs. Oetjen didn't look awfully enthusiastic the other night when Mr. Scheckner suggested we go east," Pres muttered. "I don't know, though. This is the chance of a lifetime. There's got to be a way around the authorities, right?"

But there didn't seem to be a chance. When they got to practice Tuesday afternoon, Ardith had two notes to read to them. The first was from Mrs. Oetjen and Dr. Barlow, stating unequivocally that the cheerleaders would not be excused from school for a professional advertising job, no matter what. The other was from Harris Scheckner, stating that a contract would follow. They would be filming the Clean Soap spot within the next two weeks in New York, and he would need permission slips from every parent as well as the school administrators. It would be understood that the cheerleaders would receive a fee for their services, and their expenses would be paid back to them when bills were submitted to HPS Advertising. Residuals on the commercial would be paid to them as a group after the spot started running on national television. But he needed an answer immediately. If the group was interested, they were to let him know by three P.M. the following day.

"Two weeks from now!" Mary Ellen groaned. They were all sitting with Ardith on the floor of the gym, wearing their practice clothes, not at all interested in practicing. They looked at each other in dismay.

"It's clearly impossible," Ardith stated bluntly. "We have the Wickfield and Deep River games coming up, and all that rehearsal to get in for the special cheering meet next month." She looked at their disappointed faces and shrugged. "What do you want me to do? I know how excited you all are about this, but it just isn't feasible right now. And I'm sure that if Mr. Scheckner likes you as much as he says he does, he'll keep you in mind for more work. Maybe this summer — who knows," she added hopefully.

"Madison Avenue doesn't work like that, Mrs. Engborg," Walt muttered. Since his parents ran a local TV talk show in Tarenton, he was somewhat more aware of what went on in the media than most. "When they want you, they call you. And if you don't jump when you're called, they forget you. It's as simple as that."

"There must be a way around this." Nancy was practically begging. "I mean, I know we've never missed a game, but surely the Pompon Squad could fill in for us. And we'd make up the schoolwork — honestly."

The others nodded their agreement, and Pres got down on his hands and knees in front of Ardith. "Let us go, Coach! We'll never ask anything of you again. Don't spoil our chances of success, glitter, big time!" He bowed with a flourish before her, but it didn't seem to sway Ardith one bit.

She looked at them sadly. In one way, she felt they deserved the break, and it was horribly unfair. In another, she wondered whether going to New York was such a good idea for these particular six kids. Each one of them wanted something he or she couldn't have out of life. If they saw the bright lights of New York, wouldn't it make them resent their small-town life? And what if they got hurt by this experience in some way?

Would they know how to take it? They were pretty sheltered, living in Tarenton. None of them had any street smarts at all.

"It's not my decision, kids. But Mr. Scheckner did say he needs permission slips from your parents. I suppose, if they all agreed, they might be able to override the principal's decision."

Unfortunately, the parents were united. Only Mr. and Mrs. Manners thought it might be an interesting experience for their son to go to New York and film a commercial. Anyhow, the Manners' show, *Breakfast at Home*, took up most of their lives, and they let Walt alone. Whatever he wanted to do was generally okay with them.

The Evanses were opposed on the grounds that Olivia always got lightheaded in airplanes. Mrs. Poletti decided that Angie was needed at home and couldn't be spared. Pres's father, who had deemed cheerleading a subversive activity, thought that anything connected with furthering his son's interest in it was wrong. Anyway, there were too many weirdos he might meet in New York. Nancy's parents were understanding, but they didn't like the idea of her interrupting her studies to spend a week in New York. Anyway, they'd never heard of this advertising company and doubted that it was completely aboveboard. That left Mary Ellen. Mr. and Mrs. Kirkwood simply couldn't see why this kind of thing was so important to her. They knew she had a dream of going to New York one day, but they assumed she'd outgrow it. It was just a foolish notion, after all.

"Any luck?" Pres demanded when they all met

in front of Mrs. Oetjen's office before the bell had rung for class the next morning. "We're supposed to give Mr. Scheckner an answer by three today."

"Zilch," Olivia muttered. "Anybody else?"

There was silence. They'd all struck out. And as if that weren't bad enough, Vanessa Barlow was strolling down the hall toward them, a smug smile on her face.

"Let's move it before she can come over and gloat." Nancy looked menacingly at the other girl. As they started to walk away, the principal appeared from her office, and they were hemmed in. Vanessa was about to be witness to their total failure.

"Oh, I'm glad to see you," Mrs. Oetjen nodded. "Mr. Scheckner called my office this morning, and I was just going to return his call. I think you're all aware I have to tell him that my answer is no. I don't want arguments, Walt," she went on when Walt opened his mouth to speak. "It's just a fact. You can't cut off your schoolwork and extracurricular obligations at this point. It's delightful to know that a New York firm is impressed with your cheering, but if they really wanted you, I'm sure they could have managed to film their commercial in Tarenton. Walt. . . ." She gave him a warning look. Mrs. Oetjen didn't like to be interrupted.

He'd been about to tell her why they couldn't do that. Why the client had to okay them, why they couldn't afford to transport all that equipment from their New York studio, etc. But what good would it do? Her mind was made up.

"It's so sad," Vanessa sighed. "Now Harris will go find some other kids, and they'll get all the goodies." She gave the squad members a mock-sympathetic smile. "And to think you're all missing the chance to make it big. Oh, well, better luck next time." She tossed her dark hair over one shoulder and turned so that the principal couldn't see her give them all the meanest sneer imaginable. Walt sneered back.

"All right," Mrs. Oetjen said as the bell rang. "Let's get to class, shall we? And this afternoon, at practice, I expect you to do what you've always done. Be terrific!"

With leaden feet, the six cheerleaders split up and started walking. Each of them was thinking about Mrs. Oetjen picking up that phone and dialing the number of Harris Scheckner's motel.

Mary Ellen had dreamed about going to New York and becoming a model for so long, she could almost taste what the city would be like. She just knew she would fit in, that it would become part of her as quickly as cheering had.

Nancy's brow was furrowed. She needed to get away. The relationship with Ben was so intense, so difficult at times. It wasn't that she didn't love him, but sometimes she wanted to be apart from him.

Pres felt disappointed, too. For him, New York was an out, a way to get out from under his father's thumb. And then there were his worries about Claudia. If he was running around the city, he couldn't think about that girl who'd started a fever running inside him. He didn't always deal well with gut feelings — they made him want to escape.

In history class, Mr. Demarest asked, "Does anybody have any bright ideas about the causes of World War I?" He was striding around, pointing at the map that hung off the blackboard, when there was a horrible screech, then a rhythmic clanking that could have been heard a mile away.

"What the — ?" Mr. Demarest grimaced as he strode to the door of his classroom. He seemed more perturbed about the fact that his discussion of the First World War had been disrupted than about the fact that the sound was unbearable.

"The boiler," Mary Ellen mouthed to Nancy. As soon as the ruckus began, she had gone to join several other kids at the door behind their teacher. Pres came over, shielding his ears with his hands.

"That thing is the worst!" he exclaimed. Everyone was now shouting over the hullabaloo, and going out into the hall where students and teachers from other classes were congregating. It was clearly impossible to do any work with *that* going on.

"When are they going to fix the stupid thing?" Nancy demanded.

Mary Ellen shook her head. "What did you say?"

"I said— " Nancy screamed. And then, as quickly as it had begun, the noise stopped dead. Nancy gulped. "I guess they fixed it," she continued in a normal voice.

"All right, all right." Mr. Demarest began herding his stray sheep back inside the classroom. "That's enough, now. Let's get on with our work, shall we?" He marched back to the blackboard and waited for everyone to sit down.

And then, just as the period was about to end, the loudspeaker system crackled to life. There was the sound of someone clearing her throat, and then Mrs. Oetjen's voice permeated the air. "May I have your attention?"

Everyone was silent, waiting for the explanation that was sure to come.

"I'm sorry to interrupt your classes, everybody." The principal's voice vibrated with annoyance. "This is important. I'm sure you're all impatient to know what was making all that racket a little while ago. Well, it was the old boiler again. We've just had the janitor down in the basement checking out the damage, and I'm afraid it's significant."

There was a ripple of excited interest in the classroom.

"Mr. Avery tells me that we have some exceedingly bad problems. In his exact words, 'The burner has reached the end of its useful career,' which means that we'll have to have it replaced. Unfortunately, the age of the boiler is such that parts are not readily available. It's going to take several days to receive and install the new burner."

Every eye in Mr. Demarest's class was glued to the tan mesh loudspeaker box above the blackboard. Every student knew exactly what was coming.

"Consequently, the boiler will be shut down, and I don't really think the weather is going to cooperate with us. Because it will be too cold in here to attend classes until we get the new burner in and fired up, I'm closing the school until next Wednesday."

The cheer that went up throughout the school threatened to blow the roof off Tarenton High. It was useless for Mrs. Oetjen to continue her speech, because nobody was listening. And it was equally useless for teachers to try to finish up the class they were in the middle of, because kids were jumping out of their seats, laughing and talking nonstop. The hallways were suddenly packed with liberated students, ready for their impromptu holiday.

Mary Ellen, Pres, and Nancy looked at each other, and the same thought dawned at the same time. They picked up their books and joined the throng, rushing down the hall, to find Walt, Angie, and Olivia. As soon as they saw the other squad members, they all started talking at once.

"You know what this means?" Walt crowed, throwing his arms around Olivia and giving her a very loud, very public kiss.

"It means we can do the commercial. We've got it! We won!" Angie shook her head with the wonder of it all.

"When do we leave?" Pres chuckled. "And would you like an airplane, or would you prefer to fly there unassisted?" he asked Nancy, who was literally jumping for joy.

"Wait a sec! Where's Mr. Scheckner's number?" Walt demanded.

Olivia flung the contents of her purse on the floor and pawed through the collection of junk — a hairbrush, a notepad, a pair of tights, a roll of mints, a bottle of nailpolish — until she found her wallet. Harris Scheckner's cream-colored card was sticking out of the side. "Let's go call him," she grinned, racing down the hall for the stairs to the phone bank.

"New York, here we come!" Mary Ellen said, doing a little dance in place.

There was no stopping them. The cheerleaders were about to embark on the biggest adventure of their lives so far.

CHAPTER

With the boiler on their side, the squad finally managed to coerce their parents into agreeing to the New York trip. Mrs. Evans was more than a little upset, but even she gave in after Olivia threatened to run away from home — without her hat and muffler. The other parents saw there was no way out, and actually put together a week-in-New York-plus-mad-money fund. At the last minute, it was decided that Patrick should go, too. Mrs. Oetjen simply couldn't let the group triumph in New York and not have pictures of it for the yearbook, so the staff photographer had to accompany the group. He was all too happy to oblige.

Harris Scheckner had left scripts for them as he boarded an early plane back to New York, and he instructed Ardith, who was to be the chaperone, to drill her cheerleaders until they knew the Clean Soap jingle so well they could sing it in their sleep. The cheerleaders left Tarenton the very next day in a flurry of good wishes and impossible demands. Susan Yardley wanted an I-Love-New-York T-shirt, and that was easy enough, but the Eismar twins wanted something "really punk" and Ben asked for a present from the sleaziest part of Forty-second Street. Everyone who wanted a gift donated an approximate amount, and most of the members of the senior class chipped in a little so that the squad wouldn't have to be quite so careful about how they spent their parents' money. The six team members were hysterical by Thursday afternoon. It was too much, all at once.

"I don't trust myself with all this cash," Walt said as they pushed their bags through the X-ray machine at the airport.

"Me, neither," Nancy said. "I'm sure that after a day in the city, I won't know where my head is, let alone my purse."

"Listen," Pres suggested, ushering Mary Ellen and Olivia ahead of him in line, "the only one of us who's totally trustworthy in a crisis is Angie. Let's give the dough to her." He reached for his wallet.

"Are you kidding?" Angie was flabbergasted.

"That's a terrific idea," Patrick agreed, handing over his roll of bills. The others quickly followed suit.

"Here, take it!" Olivia grimaced. "I don't want to have to deal with it anymore."

Angie looked at the wads of money, then shrugged. "If you guys really want — "

"We do!" Mary Ellen insisted. "Just put it

somewhere safe, will you? And we'll stick to you at all times, so if we need anything, you'll be available."

"And so will the cash," Walt pointed out. "Whew, what a load off my mind."

"How about keeping it with my makeup?" Angie asked, pulling the big plastic flowered case out of her purse. "Nobody'd ever suspect that."

"Sounds fine to me," Pres nodded. "Oh, boy, look who's coming." They all turned to see the familiar flag of dark, lustrous hair waving neatly over the collar of Vanessa's antique raccoon coat. "Let's get our seats before she gets on board."

The only sour note to the trip was that Vanessa was coming, too. After all, she'd told her father, one chaperone probably wasn't enough for seven kids, and her mother wasn't doing anything that week, anyway. So why didn't he send Mrs. Barlow (and Vanessa, of course) to make sure that things went smoothly?

She got her way. Vanessa generally did.

"Hi, guys!" She signaled to them, rushing ahead of her mother at the boarding gate. "Isn't this just fabulous? I plan to buy out the stores as soon as I hit town. You poor children, of course, will be so busy filming your commercial, you probably won't get to see a thing. But don't worry — I'll give you a full report on the trip home."

"Well, Van, it's not your fault Harris Scheckner doesn't want you," Walt shrugged. "Some got talent," he went on, indicating his friends, "and some — " he leered nastily at her — "some just go shopping."

Vanessa's dark eyes narrowed as she glared at him. "It may interest you to know that Harris asked me to do a solo spot first. Before he decided he needed a team effort. He has me in mind for other projects, later on," she lied.

"See," Walt smiled as the line for boarding started to move. "What'd I tell you? Roach motels."

Vanessa hurried on board with her mother, and they didn't hear a thing from her again until the plane touched down, three hours and twenty minutes later, at New York's LaGuardia Airport. They all realized that it would be impossible to fit everyone into one taxi, so Mrs. Barlow, Ardith, Vanessa, and the ever-gallant Patrick (who said he didn't really mind riding with Vanessa as long as he didn't have to sit next to her) and his camera equipment piled into the first cab in line. The second, a big old taxi, pulled up for the six cheerleaders.

"Everybody got the jingle memorized?" Mary Ellen asked as the cab sat behind about a hundred other cars trying to get through the Queens-Midtown Tunnel.

"Let's give it a run-through," Angie suggested.

"Da-da, da-da, DA-*DA!*" Pres sang by way of intro.

> "Clean, Clean is bubble,
> Clean, Clean is pure.
> Won't give your skin trouble,
> That's for sure.

"Wash your face,
Wash it with Clean.
Your skin will be the best,
That it's ever been.
Make it Clean . . .
Get it Clean . . .
You'll be Clean!"

They heard a chuckle, then a snort of laughter as they came to a rousing finish. Their cabdriver was amused and curious about their performance. "This is something." He shook his head wonderingly. "I have never been serenaded in the middle of a traffic jam by passengers. I thank you, one and all."

As the traffic inched its way forward, the six voices blended in song a second time, and the cabbie joined in at the end. He was a small, dark man wearing a squashed tweed wool cap. The shield on his much-decorated dashboard read, "Mr. T. Ghali."

"Where you folks from?" Mr. Ghali asked.

"You probably never heard of it. It's a small town in the Midwest called Tarenton. Up in the snow belt," Olivia explained.

"Nope. Can't say I have. But then, I've never been out of New York." The driver shrugged.

"Really!" Angie marveled. "We've never been out of Tarenton."

"So you've come to see the big city, sing some songs, have some fun?" He nodded, pulling abruptly across two lanes of traffic on Third Avenue so that he could make a right turn. The group — except for Pres, who drove this way himself — all gasped.

"Well, actually," Walt boasted when he could breathe again, "we're making a commercial for soap.

> "Clean, Clean is trouble,
> One thing is sure.
> Your skin will look like rubble,
> If you wash with this manure."

Walt laughed hysterically at his own rude lyrics.

"Oh, that's just great!" Nancy declared. "Don't let Harris hear you sing your version."

"I like that one," nodded Mr. Ghali, zooming up Avenue of the Americas through the staggered green lights. "More like the truth, anyway. You know what they make soap out of, don't you? Horses' hooves."

Angie, Olivia, and Walt exchanged glances. "That's pretty gross," Walt agreed. "I guess it be-*hooves* us to be honest about our product."

The others groaned at the pun.

"Well, here you are, kids," Mr. Ghali said, jamming on the brakes in front of the large chrome-and-glass hotel on Seventh Avenue and Fifty-first Street. "Have a great time. And be careful, understand? This city is a terrific place, but not everybody in it is so friendly. Got it?"

They piled out of the cab and looked around them as Mr. Ghali unloaded their luggage from the trunk. New York was something, all right. The first thing they noticed was how fast everyone walked, as though they all had urgent appointments for which they were already twenty minutes late. The second thing was the noise level.

The next thing that was remarkable was the clothing. People were dressed in every imaginable style, from high fashion to straight business to terribly sloppy to downright bizarre.

"It's like being in the middle of a really wild party," Pres commented.

"I love it!" Mary Ellen breathed, taking in the myriad unusual elements that made up one incredible experience. They walked into the hotel lobby, a giant long hall done in peach and brown. There were two mammoth chandeliers hanging over the registration desk, where Ardith and Patrick were waiting for them.

"Isn't New York wonderful?" Mary Ellen said, running to Patrick. "It kind of ropes you in, makes you participate. You can't hang back from it." She was nearly knocked over by a harried man rushing past her with two attaché cases, but Patrick neatly swept her aside in the nick of time.

"I don't know," Patrick said, holding her around the waist just in case of another imminent collision. "Look at all the garbage piled up outside. In Tarenton, we get it out of the way immediately. And the way people throw their papers and stuff down on the sidewalks. They never get this city cleaned up."

"Maybe a bar of Clean Soap would do it," Walt suggested, staggering toward the elevators with his and Olivia's bags. He was relieved when a bellhop snatched them away from him.

Ardith handed the man the keys to their rooms with a weary grin. "I don't know about you kids, but I'm beat. I really need to lie down for a while." One look at their faces told her that none of her group intended to sleep the entire time they were in New York. "Well, go on, then. But stay together, and don't talk to strangers."

"Yes, ma'am," Walt said with a solemn salute. They all turned and started for the exit.

"Wait a second," Ardith called back. "Do you have any idea at all where you're going?"

The cheerleaders looked a little sheepish, then shrugged. "Not actually," Nancy admitted. "But it's pretty easy, isn't it? I mean, the city's a grid and one number follows the next. We can't get too lost if we stay in the neighborhood."

Ardith reached into her purse for the street map she'd been given at the front desk. "Look at this once in a while, would you? And I expect you all back here by nine. We have an early call at the rehearsal studio, and I want you warmed up and ready to roll before breakfast. And have fun!" she barked at them as they ran for the revolving front door just as quickly as any New Yorker.

"Where do we start?" Mary Ellen demanded, her eyes hungrily devouring the street in front of her.

"Fifth Avenue," Angie answered at once. "I want to see the shop windows."

"Sounds perfect to me," Nancy grinned. She took the map from Walt and pointed. "If we start this way and cut over. . . ."

"You guys go ahead," Walt said. "Livvy and I have a date for a carriage ride in Central Park." He rumpled his girl friend's hair and drew her close to him. "Supposed to be pretty romantic."

"Romance, huh!" Pres grimaced. He glanced around him, feeling lost and lonely. He didn't really want to window-shop, and he certainly wasn't going to horn in on his friends' date.

"We've been planning this for a week," Olivia explained, her dark eyes gleaming. "See you guys back here later."

"Okay, girls," Patrick sang out, slinging his Pentax over one shoulder. "Fifth Avenue it is, if you insist. C'mon, Pres." He took Mary Ellen's hand and started down the street.

"Naw, I don't really want to check out stores," Pres shrugged. "I thought I might take a subway and get off in Greenwich Village, maybe grab something to eat. See you." He stuck his hands in his pockets and turned away from them, vanishing around the next corner.

Angie shook her head. "I'm worried about him. Ever since Claudia left for California, he's been awfully moody."

"Wouldn't you be?" Nancy demanded, glancing down at the map. "That girl's in such danger, and Pres really seems to love her." She shook her head and started walking. "I just hope it doesn't spoil the trip for him."

"Not Pres," Patrick said. "That guy doesn't stay down for long."

"He does," Mary Ellen disagreed. "He just doesn't let anyone know it when he's miserable." She had dated Pres off and on, and knew him pretty well. He was the proverbial poor little rich boy, someone who could smile on the outside and be crying on the inside.

They walked down Fifth Avenue, checking out the clothes in windows, the people on the street, the very taste of sooty air, and the smells of exotic food, from Greek souvlaki to Chinese noodles, being cooked on little carts up and down the avenue. They looked up more than they looked down, admiring the spires of St. Patrick's Cathedral, the looming skyscrapers farther downtown, and the hazy light that grew pinker and darker as time passed.

"What a sky!" Mary Ellen grinned at the sunset.

"It's the pollution," Patrick told her firmly.

"It is not." She felt magical tonight, a Cinderella unleashed on the world of fairy tales and dreams come true.

Patrick insisted. "Toxic waste from New Jersey." He looked at her face and he knew, just as surely as he knew how beautiful she was, that New York would swallow her alive. He wanted her to stay with him in Tarenton, and yet he cared for her enough to want her to choose that life for herself. He only wished he could tell her that in a way that she might understand. If she fell in love with the city at first sight and came rushing back here after graduation, she was destined to be unhappy. But no one could tell her that — she would have to find out for herself.

As their friends were absorbing the sights and sounds of Fifth Avenue, Walt and Olivia were just getting to the carriage stand in front of the Plaza Hotel.

"We need one that looks really authentic," Walt said decisively, yanking Olivia up to a cab with a sad-looking black horse wearing a wreath of silk flowers on his ears. The driver was a young guy, maybe in his early twenties, dressed to the hilt in a top hat and a cutaway coat. "Hi," Walt said to the driver as he helped Olivia up onto the high seat. "Once around the park," he told the man loftily.

"Maybe you better ask how much, Walt," Olivia whispered when the driver just sat there, eyeing the two kids carefully as if he was trying to figure out their monetary worth. "Did you give all your cash to Angie?" she asked nervously.

"It's seventeen bucks for the first half hour," the driver said coolly. "And five bucks more every fifteen minutes after that. The seventeen has to be paid up front," he added.

"What?" Walt said, totally losing his casualness.

"That's incredible." Olivia shook her head. She started to climb down. "Let's forget about it and just take a walk, okay?"

"Absolutely not," Walt told her, pushing her back down in the upholstered seat. Then he fished in his back pocket and came up with a crumpled five-dollar bill. He found five more ones in his front pocket. "How about a twenty-minute ride?" he asked the driver. "Seeing as how it's winter and you don't have that many customers."

The guy looked at him sharply, then shrugged.

"You're from way out of town, right? Like the moon."

"No. Tarenton," Olivia said primly, waiting for him to insult their hometown.

"Tarenton, sure. Might as well be the moon." The guy shrugged. "I was from out of town myself once," he said, softening. Then he urged the horse forward. Walt and Olivia sat back, their arms around each other. New York was full of surprises and adventures, and they were having both.

CHAPTER

Pres walked over to Broadway and eyed the entrance to the IRT. Was this the right train to the Village? He didn't want to look stupid by asking somebody, but he didn't want to get too lost right away. The city was pretty awesome, just as his parents had said it was. His father came here on business occasionally, and he'd offered to take his son along once or twice, but Pres had declined, figuring it was just a ploy to get him involved in Tarenton Fabricators. If there was one thing he didn't want, it was to inherit his father's business (i.e., his father's headaches). Anyhow, even New York wasn't worth having to spend all that time with a parent.

But to be alone in this incredible city, that was really ideal. Pres didn't know what he wanted in his future, but there was something about the race of his pulse as he walked down the crowded streets, the feeling of success in the air that made him heady with possibility. Maybe, when Claudia recovered, they could pool their resources and move here for a year. She could work and he . . . well, he'd come up with some terrific business venture. He'd market a product that everybody would have to have, like Pet Rocks or chocolate-covered kiwis. They might even be able to save money by taking an apartment with Mary Ellen, while she got her modeling career off the ground. And then, at the end of a year, Pres could come back to Tarenton and show his father exactly what he had accomplished, all by himself. It would be —

"Hey, watch it, buddy." A low, mellow female voice woke him from his daydream. "Well," she continued, staring at him intently, "are you going down those stairs or do you plan to stand here and wait for the ball to drop in Times Square next New Year's Eve?" She laughed at him, a low, husky laugh.

"I . . . ah . . . I was just going to take the subway," he explained casually, looking at the incredible vision before him. She was very petite, a scaled-down model of everything feminine. Her dark curly hair hugged her neat little head; her rosebud lips puckered appealingly over a determined chin that she stuck out when she talked. She wore gold earrings in the shape of lightning bolts that shook a little when she moved. She was thin but muscular, and amazingly curvy in all the right places. Her dark eyes, accented by darker makeup, were savvy and amused — they made her look older than her years. She was probable his age, maybe a year or two older.

And there was no doubt about the fact that she was a dyed-in-the-wool New Yorker. You could tell by her accent, and naturally, by her clothes. She had on high, black, flat-heeled riding boots, into which old, faded jeans were neatly tucked. She was wrapped in a voluminous red cape with padded shoulders, and the giant garment nearly swallowed her up. Made her look kind of cute, though.

"Don't tell me," she grinned, raising a gloved hand to the air in a graceful gesture. "You're on your way to Greenwich Village."

"How'd you know that?" Pres asked skeptically, certain she was making fun of him.

"Well. . . ." She leaned on the subway banister, crossing her arms and legs. "Let's put it this way. I can tell by the way you sort of stare down these steps like there's a weird monster lurking, that you've never taken a subway before. Which means you're a tourist. Which means you're either bound for the Village or the Empire State Building or the World Trade Center. And I just had a hunch about the Village. You look like the type."

"What type is that?" Pres was fascinated by her. The girls in Tarenton didn't come on to strangers this way, as if they were in charge. She was intriguing, like a good mystery where you don't know who dunnit until the very end.

"You are repressed, bothered, and bewildered," she told him bluntly. "Probably can't stand your father. Am I right?"

When he laughed and nodded, she clapped her hands in delight. "My parents are both shrinks, but I'm the best diagnostician in the family."

"Shrinks. You mean headshrinkers. Psychiatrists — both of them?" Pres knew a couple of kids at school who'd had therapy, and his mother had once even suggested that he "talk to somebody," as she euphemistically put it. But he'd never seriously considered it. Psychiatrists were grown-ups, and therefore, suspect.

"Both of them." She shrugged. "Say, forget the Village. You can do that some other time. Just come with me to the nearest pretzel vendor. I didn't eat lunch and I'm absolutely famished. Look, I know this city like the back of my hand — I won't steer you wrong. You can trust me. What do you say?" she asked with ease.

He shook his head at her.

"What's the matter?"

Pres didn't like to admit that anybody else handled situations with more aplomb than he did, but here was this girl, who hadn't even introduced herself, about to drag him off to eat pretzels without even worrying about who he was or what his intentions were. She was amazing. "Don't you even want to know my name?"

"Uh-uh. Just your Social Security number." She made a face at him. "Oh, well, if you're determined to be conventional . . . I'm Blake. C'mon, my stomach won't hold out a minute longer."

She took his arm and yanked him across Broadway toward Seventh Avenue, making a beeline for the vendor on the corner. Smoke rose from his cart into the still air, and the sweet scent of chestnuts wafted toward them as they approached him.

"Two pretzels, with extra salt," Blake told the vendor. "Pay the man," she instructed Pres.

This girl was something! "How much?" he inquired, reaching into his pocket for the few bills he had.

"Oh, great, I can see you're loaded." She scoffed at his skimpy stash. "That'll be two dollars, if you don't think it'll bust you. I better take you to one of my New-York-on-a-shoestring sights. Very good, very cheap."

Munching her pretzel, she pulled him along down the block. When they came to the Exxon Building on Fiftieth Street, she hurried him east toward Avenue of the Americas. To his surprise, right in the middle of offices and stores was a little pocket park.

"This way." She smiled when she saw the look on his face. They walked under a concrete arch off which cascades of water rippled in pretty patterns. The sound of a rushing waterfall was totally inconguous with the background of traffic, Pres thought, but it was very welcome. "Take a seat," she offered, pointing to the neat arrangement of chairs around artfully placed bushes. The park extended across three city blocks. A variety of street people, tired business types, and kids were hanging around, eating or reading newspapers, generally enjoying the respite from the pace of the city.

Pres took a bite of his pretzel and chewed for

a moment, savoring the doughy, salty taste. "Do you pick up guys often? I mean, I could have been a mugger — or worse."

She gave him a skeptical look. "Listen, I've lived in this city all my life, and I can smell a mugger a mile away. You are just too . . . innocent. Anyhow, I have a brown belt in karate. I don't really think I'm in any danger." She smiled, and looked at him indulgently.

Pres was more than a little upset at her impression of him. Back home, nobody would have said he was anything but sophisticated — maybe even a little dangerous. "My name is Pres, by the way. Pres Tilford. And I'm sure you've never heard of Tarenton, where I'm from, but — "

"Pres, now that's unusual. Stands for. . . ?"

"Preston."

She pounded her thigh with her fist. "I knew it! Incredible! That has to be your father's name, too, right? Nobody in their right mind would give a kid a name like Preston if it weren't in the family. You're Preston, Jr., aren't you?"

He flushed. "Worse than that. The third. You know an awful lot." Then he went on. "Bet you don't know why I'm in New York, though."

"You won an all-expenses-paid vacation to the Big Apple. Contest at your local supermarket. No?" She shrugged gamely when he shook his head. "No, you're here to interview for college." She grimaced when he kept smiling, knowing that he'd stumped her. "You punched out your phys ed teacher and you're on the lam."

He polished off the end of his pretzel, then folded his arms. "You know something? You've

54

got a weird mind. Well, the real answer is that I'm on the Varsity Cheerleading Squad at school, and we were discovered by this ad guy. We're filming a commercial for Clean Soap. Staying at the Sheraton for the week."

Her face changed abruptly. "You're not. *Please*, tell me you're not really a cheerleader." She got up to leave, dusting the salt off her gloves. "That's repulsive."

Pres stood up, towering over her. "Thanks a lot. I needed that." He usually got a kick out of people's reactions to his choice of extracurricular activity, but for some reason, it annoyed him to be put down by this girl.

"Oh, come on." She put a hand on his arm, but it didn't soothe his ruffled feathers one bit. "I just meant . . . well, people in New York don't do that. Only air heads become cheerleaders. Don't take offense, that's just the way it is. But I suppose in Tarkington — "

"Tarenton," he corrected her brusquely.

"Whatever. Listen, you do your thing, and I do mine." She extended her hand to him, suddenly very cool. "Nice to meet you. Have a great time in New York, okay?" She drew her cape around her more tightly, then started to walk away.

"Wait a second." Pres exhaled deeply, then decided it wasn't worth it to just let her run off. She was fun and interesting and it totally hurt his male pride to have *her* walk out on *him*. He stuck out his hand, offering her a truce. "I'd really like to see you again, Blake. Ah, Blake. . . ?"

"Norton," she told him.

"Well, I'm only here for a week, Blake Norton, but we could have a meal, go for a walk. . . ." He reached for something that would appeal to her. "Why don't you give me your number?"

She laughed, then shrugged. "Why not? But if you're only going to be here a week, it's stupid to go through the formalities of calling and making dates. I'll pick you up at your hotel — say tomorrow night at seven? I'll wear a flower in my lapel," she grinned, "so you'll remember who I am. You can introduce me to all your other cheerleader friends." She tried hard not to sound sarcastic.

And then, as though she had known him all her life, she kissed him casually on the cheek and walked off, happy to have impressed the daylights out of him.

He walked back to his hotel slowly, going over their conversation again in his head. It was only after he was back in the room he was sharing with Walt and Patrick, lying on the bed, looking up at the ceiling, that he realized he hadn't thought about Claudia for four hours straight.

"I can't take this anymore! I absolutely cannot!" Vanessa paced the floor, digging into the plush burgundy carpeting with her heels, as though she wanted to hurt it.

"Now, dear, calm down." Mrs. Barlow tried to soothe her daughter.

"But they're just so awful to me. They think they're all so wonderful, so exceptional, just because Harris picked them for that dumb commercial. Last night, after they all came back here and we were sitting around in the lobby, they totally snubbed me. Waltzed right past us with Mrs. Engborg, just like we weren't here. I heard them say they were going out for ice cream sodas at Rumpelmayer's. Ooh, it gets me so furious!" She threw herself down dramatically on the bed and pulled her uncombed hair over her face. "I'll show them," she muttered, so that her mother couldn't hear.

"But we have such a lovely day planned, dear," Mrs. Barlow reminded her. "Shopping at Bloomingdale's, lunch at that nice French place your father heard about, the Metropolitan Museum of Art, and then dinner and a Broadway show. You'll forget all about what your friends are doing."

"Fat chance," Vanessa murmured, getting up to look at herself in the mirror. She was still brooding about her confrontation the night before with the six people she hated most in the world.

They had all come in about nine, positively glowing, Walt and Olivia with their arms wrapped around each other, Mary Ellen and Patrick mooning into each other's eyes. Angie and Nancy couldn't stop talking about everything they'd seen, and Pres, completely silent, had looked right through her. They were so disgustingly happy, so smug about being a group and being the chosen ones. And when she'd suggested that Harris might change his mind about using them when he saw them next to all those professional kids he dealt with for most of his commercials, they had just laughed at her.

Laughed at her — at Vanessa Barlow! At least

back home when she said something to them, the barbs usually hit their mark. But here, for some reason, they were impervious to her attempts, protected by their cheerleader groupiness.

The expression on her face slowly changed from miserable to thoughtful to canny. She had an idea, one that just might work. "Wait a second — just a minute." She ran to the bureau for her purse and fished out Harris Scheckner's business card. "Perfect!" she exclaimed. "This'll be super."

Scheckner and his choreographer, a thin, nervous man named Dan Moore who chain-smoked long, brown cigarettes, were sitting in the studio over their third cups of coffee when the phone rang.

"Harris? Hi. This is Vanessa Barlow — you remember, the superintendent of schools' daughter from Tarenton? Remember how I said if I was ever in New York, I wanted to audition for you? Well, it just so happens that I'm here. I know you're about to start rehearsals, but could I see you this morning? Just for a second?"

When Vanessa placed the receiver back down, she was smiling. "You go to Bloomingdale's without me, Mom," she said, looking at her mother's reflection in the mirror so that she could see herself, too. "I've got something to do this morning."

CHAPTER

The rehearsal studio was in an old factory building near Eleventh Avenue in the Forties. The streets were busy despite the desolate look of the neighborhood, with trucks barreling over the potholes, and workmen manipulating jackhammers on the cracked concrete.

"Sure doesn't look like home," Angie said, grinning as they pulled open the heavy metal door of the building and walked inside. The blast of cold air that hit them was damp and smelled of mold.

"Gee, I don't know. They're putting up a parking lot by the mall, aren't they?" Walt had his and Olivia's duffle bags over one shoulder and some of Patrick's camera equipment over another. "Concrete is concrete, however you slice it," he quipped. "Except you can't slice it, because it's solid, man, solid."

Nobody was listening to Walt's joke because

they were too preoccupied with their surroundings. The freight elevator had come to a stop right before them, and the elevator operator, an old man wearing ancient overalls with an ancient cigar stub hanging out of the side of his mouth, had just opened the metal gate for them.

"Floor?" he asked.

"Top floor. Seven, please," Ardith said.

"This is incredible!" Mary Ellen breathed. "I can't really believe we're here. Somebody pinch me."

Patrick grinned and reached inside the high collar of her coat to oblige. "Well, you can't call it glamorous," he reminded her.

Mary Ellen refused to be brought down to earth. "It's wonderful," she told him as the elevator clanked to a halt and the operator jimmied the handle up and down several times.

"Watch your step," he muttered when he saw that he still hadn't hit the floor exactly.

"Well, good morning!" Harris' cheery voice greeted them as they stepped into the studio.

The cheerleaders were astounded. In this grimy building, the production company had created light and airy spaces. A huge, open room with big floor-to-ceiling windows was the centerpiece of the studio, with polished hardwood floors and lighting and camera equipment everywhere. A giant vase of pussywillows and eucalyptus stood to one side of the entry hall, where a receptionist was whipping out letters on a fancy-looking electronic typewriter. She glanced up at them, nodded, and went back to her work.

"Kids, great to see you," Harris said, hustling

them inside. "This is our choreographer, Dan Moore. Dan, these are the cheerleaders of Tarenton High, for your inspection. And this is Casey, my assistant; Peaches, the greatest rehearsal pianist known to man; Tony, who works the lights; Elio on camera; and Jock, our jack of all trades, otherwise known as a gofer. Why don't you just change and we'll get to work. Everybody know the jingle?"

They murmured their assent and let Casey lead them into two dressing rooms with real professional makeup lights around the banks of wall mirrors.

"I think I have died and gone to heaven," Mary Ellen sighed as Casey closed the door behind her.

"Do you think it'll be hard?" Nancy asked nervously, brushing her silky brown hair with deliberation. "Do you think we'll be able to do it?"

"We can do anything," Mary Ellen proclaimed, looking as starry-eyed as she felt. She had hardly slept the previous night, as visions of places to go and things to do had danced in her head. And she'd been up at dawn with the telephone directory, jotting down the names and numbers of modeling agencies to call at her first opportunity.

"I've always wanted a mirror like this," Olivia confessed, peering at herself as she pulled her light brown hair into a ponytail.

"Hey, come on over to my mom's beauty parlor," Angie laughed, pulling on her tights. "We've got them in droves."

"Oh, Angie," Mary Ellen clucked. "It's not the *same*."

The boys were waiting for them when they came out, sitting with Dan Moore and Ardith in front of one of the windows.

"Okay, ready or not. . . ." Dan got them on their feet. Then he turned to Patrick, who was standing with Ardith, just waiting. "You! You want to take a couple of snapshots of your friends, is that it?"

Patrick grinned, ignoring the man's patronizing tone. "Something like that, yes."

"Okay, just stay out of range of my cameras, understand? The minute you're underfoot, you're out." He turned back to the group. "Can I see something you've prepared?" he asked. "Just to give me an idea of what I'm working with." He said this as though he was expecting the worst. He was clearly letting them know that he resented working with amateurs, no matter how good they were purported to be.

"Why don't you show Dan that halftime routine we worked up for the Northfield game?" Ardith suggested. "Mary Ellen, start them off with the 'Pride' and 'Tiger' cheers, and go on from there. Start over there, in the center, and — "

"Ah, excuse me, Mrs. Engborg." Dan came around and placed Mary Ellen where he wanted her. "I'll take over now, thanks." He began to group the kids on the right side of the room. Ardith stood next to him, looking a little puzzled and more than a little miffed. "Just, ah, do anything. It doesn't matter much — I only want to see how you move."

Mary Ellen looked over at Ardith, but her

62

coach had walked around to the back of the piano and was very busily staring out the window. "Okay, gang," she said gamely, "One, two. . . ."

> "We've got pride,
> Got vigor and vim,
> We've got the team
> That's gonna win!"

She cartwheeled around the floor, then let Pres lift her to a stand and swoop her up to his shoulders as Walt did the same with Angie. Nancy and Olivia came out of their pikes to make a handstand bridge, from which they tumbled into tight somersaults. They each stood up from a backbend and joined Mary Ellen in a series of herky jumps and stag leaps.

It had been at least an hour since they'd warmed up at their hotel, and the six of them were used to a lot more preparation. Also, even though they weren't really nervous, the situation was strange to them. All these people watching — not like fans at a game or judges in a competition, but rather cynical viewers, almost daring the group to be good. The result, of course, was that they gave a pretty lackluster performance.

"All right. Okay, thanks, kids." Dan lit another cigarette and went over to Harris, who was sitting over a sheaf of notes with Casey. The three of them huddled for a minute. The cheerleaders could just barely make out their conversation.

"What did I tell you?" Harris asked. "Do they have spirit or what?" He hadn't looked at them once they were in motion.

"Spirit, yeah," Dan said in a disgusted voice. "They don't have the look, Harris. You know the image we're after."

"Right, boss," Casey said. She was a rail-thin young woman with blood-red nails, wearing a hot-pink jumpsuit. "We want something snazzy for Clean Soap. Not, well. . . ." She gestured hopelessly at the cheerleaders. "Not so —" she searched for a particularly dull image — "so white bread."

"They don't like us," Pres commented.

"So? I don't like them much myself," Walt muttered.

"Shut up, you two," Olivia warned them. "We're just the cogs in a big wheel."

"Speak for yourself," Nancy grimaced.

"You, you in the pink tights." Dan came over to the group, looking very worried. "Can you do a split?" he demanded of Angie.

"Sure. And the name's Angie," she stated firmly.

"Right. And you over there, Muscles," he addressed Walt. "Can you lift the little girl while you're in this position?" He demonstrated, taking Olivia by one hand and catapulting her over his shoulder as he half lay on the floor.

"Yeah, I guess, but — "

"No buts," Dan counseled Walt. "Peaches, let's have a little music, shall we?" The choreographer stood up in front of the group and got down in a crouch.

"You, the pretty one," he beckoned to Mary Ellen. "Follow me." He snapped his fingers for a beat, then demonstrated a jazzy sequence of steps that went very fast. "Got that?"

"I think so." She did as he asked, feeling terribly strange. No one had ever talked to them this way.

"Not like that." He ran his hands over his face, then rushed over to his ashtray for a puff of the cigarette. "Try it again."

"Lift your leg in the turn, Mary Ellen," Ardith suggested.

Dan bit his lower lip, then walked over to their coach. "I think it may be more helpful, Mrs. Engborg, if you just leave the direction to me."

Ardith's back went up. How did he dare to imply that she was in the way?

"Okay, sweetheart," Harris nodded to Mary Ellen. "Let's see that opening again."

Mary Ellen was getting angry now. First them, now Ardith. It was rude to order people around as though they were cattle. She executed the steps again, but her heart wasn't in it.

Dan sighed, motioning to the pianist. "Hold up a sec. Harris, where's that other girl?"

"Right. Let's give her a try." Harris walked across the huge studio to a door near the back and yanked it open. "Okay, honey."

Mary Ellen and the others let their gaze wander back toward the door. Each of them stared in disbelief. It couldn't be — it just wasn't possible!

"Vanessa, honey." Harris smiled at her indulgently, as she walked to the center of the room. "Let's see those steps we were working on this morning, okay?" She sauntered past the cheerleaders, not even bothering to give them a backwards glance. Her hair was a wild profusion of dark curls that framed her heavily made-up face. She was wearing an exotic leopard-print stretch suit, and looked very sexy.

"Oh, no," Pres ran his hands through his hair. "Wouldn't you know she'd pull something like this?" He sat down heavily on the floor, folding his arms across his chest.

"Vanessa here explained to me that she's your extra cheerleader, the girl you call in for the really tough gymnastic stuff," Harris said absent-mindedly. "Okay, sweetheart, give it a whirl."

Vanessa, who had obviously been working on the steps in the back room by herself for the past hour, put on a bravura show. She really looked as though she knew what she was doing. The slick routine looked as right on her as it had looked all wrong on Mary Ellen.

"That snake in the grass!" Olivia hissed. "She told them she was part of us! What nerve."

"And of course, she got here early enough to get some special training. She knows the number cold." Mary Ellen looked at Vanessa's body critically. Nobody would deny that she had a great figure, and that it looked wonderful in clothes. But there was something stiff about her movements, something completely phony. And yet, that seemed to be just what the guys wanted.

"Perfect!" Dan nodded when Vanessa ended the sequence with a cute little bow. "I love it. Love ya, babe. Okay, the rest of you, line up behind her. We'll give you something a little easier to try."

Humiliated beyond belief, the cheerleaders worked as a backup group for the rest of the day. The things Dan gave them to do were stagey and posed, like moving statues. After six hours of rehearsal, they were exhausted from behaving like a Las Vegas chorus line. Nobody said a word as they went down in the freight elevator at about six-thirty. They were all angry, tired, and disgusted with the stupidity of the whole deal.

"Main floor." The elevator man brought the creaking machine to a halt, and they all got out. Ardith was as silent as the rest of them, lost in a world of her own.

"So, I guess we have to start this whole thing all over again bright and early tomorrow," Angie sighed as they walked east toward Broadway.

"What's the use?" Nancy sighed. "This isn't at all how I expected it to be."

"Look, kids, you did real well," Ardith consoled them halfheartedly. "It's not your fault they had something entirely different in mind."

"Different!" Walt snorted. "Yeah, Vanessa is different all right! She doesn't even know the jingle," he grumbled, "and those guys are falling all over her."

"She knows how to get around *not* knowing the jingle," Nancy said. "And if her mother drills her on it all night, they won't be ashamed to show her to the client."

"Ashamed!" Pres threw up his hands. "I'd be ashamed to be seen on national television in back of that girl!"

They walked another block in silence, letting the city sounds drown out the loud promptings of their own consciences. They were doing something none of them believed in, and they felt awful.

"So, what do you guys want to do tonight?" Ardith asked, forcing some false enthusiasm into her voice.

"Well, there's always dinner in Chinatown or Little Italy," Angie said eagerly. Even though she was really down, the thought of food cheered her up considerably, much to her chagrin.

"And the World Trade Center is open late," Olivia offered. "What time is it, anyway?"

Pres glanced down at his watch and was about to tell her when he suddenly realized that he had a date. He smacked his forehead with the heel of his hand. "Seven P.M.! Oh, no! I said I'd meet Blake at the hotel at seven."

Walt gave him a friendly pat on the back. "Well, you win a few, lose a few, old buddy." Walt, who'd never really dated anyone other than Olivia, was always amused at Pres's interchangeable women. He'd been glad when Pres had fallen for Claudia, because the dizzying merry-go-round of girls had stopped.

"Don't you believe it," Olivia told her boyfriend. "If I know Pres, the girl will wait for him. It's his magnetic appeal," she teased him.

"Look, this isn't a date or anything," Pres said quickly, feeling guilty about Claudia already. "You people are invited."

"Oh, no," Mary Ellen said. "I'm not really up for meeting your new friend tonight." Actually, she wanted time on her own to think out her strategy for the next day. During their lunch break, she'd managed to make an appointment at one of the smaller modeling agencies. She'd hoped to get to see a few people at all the top places, but the big agencies demanded more than just a few days' notice.

"We've got our own plans," Patrick said quietly, slipping an arm around Mary Ellen's waist. She didn't remove it, but he felt her stiffen. In New York, apparently, he didn't look quite so attractive to her as he did in Tarenton.

"And I want an early night, thanks," Angie stated as they reached the door of their hotel. "I'll just dole out some money to everybody and you can go off and do your own thing."

"I'll stay with you, Angie," Ardith said gratefully. "I know I haven't done much today, but suddenly, I'm too tired to drag one foot in front of the other. Maybe early tomorrow morning we should go over the stuff Dan gave you tonight, to make sure you know it."

"We won't be late, Mrs. Engborg," Nancy told her consolingly. "We'll race up to the top of the World Trade Center and down again."

"And then see the South Street Seaport and be right back," Walt nodded. "Maybe just throw in the Trump Tower and the Empire State Building on our way."

Ardith had to laugh. "You can't wait until tomorrow, I suppose."

The group just looked at her.

"Well," their coach said, shrugging reluctantly, "you better get moving if you intend to see all of New York before dinner." What could she do? These six were unstoppable. Even a New York choreographer supplanting them with such an inferior replacement couldn't get their morale down.

"Okay, Angie," Pres said, looking around for a small, curly headed person near the hotel entrance. "I need some cash so we can get going."

Angie began to poke around in her purse, but Ardith put a hand on her arm. "Are you nuts? Never, *ever* take out your money in a public place. This is a big city," she hissed.

"Sorry," Angie flushed. "Come on inside, guys. I'll pay you there." She ran up the steps ahead of them, and paused only when she had ensconced herself in a deserted corner of the giant lobby.

"Okay, everyone, come and get it," she said, sticking her hand in her purse and rummaging around for her makeup case. She felt her wallet, and her notebook, and her gum, and hairbrush. She felt her pen and extra pair of tights. She did not feel anything else. She dumped the contents of her bag onto the nearest end table.

"It's gone!" she cried. "The case is gone!"

CHAPTER

7

"You have to be out of your mind! What are you talking about?" Nancy looked frantic.

"Oh, come on, Ange, it *has* to be here somewhere." Pres began pawing through the things that lay on the table, like the myriad pieces of an incomprehensible jigsaw puzzle.

"You must have left it upstairs, in the room," Mary Ellen said decisively.

"Didn't I see you take it out this morning, at breakfast?" Patrick asked.

Ardith shook her head, then started for the front desk. "I'll report it to the management. Maybe they'll be able to help."

"What are we going to do?" Walt exclaimed, plopping himself down on the nearest couch.

"Are you guys having a problem, or what?" The husky voice caused Pres to turn around at once. Blake Norton looked at the seven of them with an indulgent smile. She was wearing a slim navy reefer coat with a red carnation pinned to the lapel, and shiny boots.

"Oh, Blake!" Pres looked confused and disturbed. This was no way to start an evening with his new, outspoken acquaintance. "Uh, Angie here was carrying all our money in her makeup kit, and the thing's disappeared. Everybody, this is Blake Norton."

The cheerleaders nodded perfunctorily and turned their attention back to Angie.

"Think, Angie," Olivia insisted. "You must have taken it out at the studio. Could you have left it in the dressing room?"

Angie shook her head mournfully. "I didn't put on any makeup all day. I didn't have time." She closed her eyes, staunching back the flow of tears that threatened to spill out at any moment. "You guys said I was so trustworthy."

Mary Ellen put an arm around her friend. "You are, Ange. This has nothing to do with your being responsible."

"We're not blaming you," Patrick reassured her.

Blake looked at the seven of them wonderingly. "For heaven's sake," she grunted, raking one manicured hand through the pile of Angie's possessions, "you've been ripped off. Happens every day in the big city."

Walt shook his head. "But why wouldn't he have taken her wallet?"

Blake shrugged. "Who knows? Hey, don't look so down. It could have been worse."

"Yeah?" Pres rolled his eyes at her. "This happened to be all our money, plus what our parents

72

gave us to survive here for a week. All I've got now is — " he reached into his jeans pocket and came up with three dollar bills and some change — "is this!"

Blake made a face. "You people are such babes in the woods. Didn't anyone ever tell you about traveler's checks out there in Tarenton? Or credit cards?"

The seven of them felt absolutely terrible, totally unprepared for the onslaught on New York they had expected to make. First, Vanessa had made a clean sweep of their professional abilities, and now, some rip-off artist had seen to it that they wouldn't even be able to enjoy the sights of the city. Not to mention pay for their hotel bill and meals.

"Ardith has a credit card. I guess she can take care of things for a while," Nancy said solemnly.

"We've got to go to the police," Angie said nervously. "They'll be able to help."

Blake just laughed. "You have to be kidding. Come on, sweetheart, think it out for yourself. How does a police officer go about tracing your steps and finding the culprit who was just a yard behind you when your purse happened to be hanging open? It's a waste of time, guys. Why don't you let me take you all out to dinner instead?" She grinned knowledgeably. "I've got my father's credit card."

Pres muttered something and shook his head. When he'd been dating Kerry and living on his own without his parents' permission, he'd allowed her to pay for meals occasionally because he was flat broke. But he'd just met this girl, and accepting her offer would make him feel really rotten. In his world, the guy took the girl out — at least on the first date.

"No, really," he began.

"Sure, we'd love to," Walt chimed in. "I'm Walt, by the way. And this is Olivia. You've already met Angie. And Nancy and Mary Ellen and Patrick."

"Well," Blake gestured toward the hotel entrance. "Now that the formalities are over, shall we. . . ?" She looked at their downcast faces and sighed. "I can see this is going to be a real fun evening."

Angie shook her head anxiously. "I want to go to the police first."

"If you insist," Blake shrugged. "But you better check your room, and wherever else you were today. The cops are going to think you're a real boob if you haven't covered all your bases."

Angie frowned and stared at the girl. "Why are you so cynical about everything?"

"Because, my dear," Blake said in a worldly wise voice, "I am a New Yorker. Comes with the territory."

The kids ransacked the rooms and found nothing at all. Ardith had gotten no satisfaction from the hotel management. The most they had promised was that they would inform her if anything turned up. And even Angie agreed that it would be stupid to go to the police without checking the studio the next morning. It didn't really seem to make much difference now. Time was on the side of whoever had the money.

"The thing to do is stop thinking about it,"

74

Blake said calmly as she led the way to the subway stop an hour later. "Consider the cash gone, and enjoy your dinner. We're going to Soho for Thai food. That'll cheer you up."

"What food?" Angie looked dazed and troubled.

Blake had the good sense not to make fun of the girl. After all, she was in a bad way. "It's great stuff. Thousand-layer pancakes, chilis, and exotic sauces. You'll love it. At least, I can guarantee you've never had anything like it before."

"Let's do it," Walt said cheerily. He looked at the others, who nodded. "Thanks, Blake. We'll pay you back."

"Forget it. Really. Just, let's make tracks, okay?" she said, hurrying them along. "This place is jammed after eight P.M."

They descended into the subway with a horde of other people and were swept along to the turnstiles. Blake handed them each a token and, as they passed through, a train pulled into the station. The noise was deafening; a thunderous rush of metal and air that made the Tarenton High boiler sound like a pussycat's purr.

"Step lively!" Blake insisted, pushing them inside amid the crush of straphangers. "You have to move fast or the doors close on you." She grabbed Pres, who grabbed Mary Ellen, Angie, and Nancy, who hung onto Patrick for dear life.

Walt pulled Olivia in and protectively huddled about her, clutching the pole in the center for support. The subway car lurched and swayed, then eased itself into a more regular rhythm.

"Oh, boy," Pres grimaced when they were

nearly thrown to the floor. The train had decided to come to a dead halt, right in the middle of the tunnel. "Do you really ever get used to this?"

Mary Ellen grinned at him. "I kind of like it. Makes traveling a real experience. You wouldn't get bored going to work every day."

Patrick looked at the ceiling. "Is there anything about New York you don't like?" The train groaned, then churned into action once again.

Mary Ellen thought a minute, then shrugged. "Vanessa. But that's true wherever I am."

Blake studied them all as the quick journey continued, getting a real kick out of their reactions. They might be green, but they were game, at least. And they had a way of making her see her city through new eyes. The everyday things, the ones she took for granted, were special to these cheerleaders.

"Last stop — everybody out!" she yelled at Spring Street. Herding her charges quickly ahead of her, she ushered them out of the subway, up to the street. The storefronts were different here, a hodgepodge of antiques and wild clothing and art galleries and restaurants, all housed in old factory buildings. The Thai place, with colored streamers covering the narrow doorway, was just down the block. They walked into the tiny room and took seats at the round corner table, which was the only one big enough for eight.

"Ba-mee all round," Blake said expansively to the waitress. "And kung pao after that. We'll have that coconut milk drink, too, okay? I warn you," she said to the cheerleaders when the waitress had given them all chopsticks and hurried back to the kitchen with their order. "This is the hottest food in the world, so watch it."

"Good," Walt nodded. "Maybe we can burn our troubles away."

"Well, there must be a way out of this," Angie sighed. "We can call our folks and get them to wire us some more money, I suppose."

"No, that's a lousy idea," Pres said. He hated asking his father for anything, and to ask twice was too much. "Harris just has to pay us early."

"But our contract said we get the expenses back *after* the filming," Nancy pointed out.

"I think he'll give in, seeing as how this is an emergency." Patrick shrugged, looking at the strange flat pancake the waitress had just placed in front of him.

"So you people are filming a commercial," Blake said, digging in expertly with her chopsticks. "I can relate. It's like everything is selling these days, even the Midwest. Oops, sorry," she chuckled, taking a bite of her food. "I just meant, to an urban dweller like myself, *you're* the tourist attraction and the stuff you consider wild and unusual is commonplace. It just depends on your perspective."

"I see what you mean," Pres nodded, looking at her again. She was smart, alright, and it wasn't the kind of smart you got from reading books. It was gut-smart, a quality that came from deep inside.

"The thing is," Olivia was telling Blake, "we thought we were going to be the stars of this thing, and now we're just so much scenery. This awful, lousy, rotten girl we know — "

"Vanessa," Walt chimed in.

"Right, Vanessa — well, she's taken over," Olivia continued, munching a shrimp from her kung pao. "Has the director and choreographer wrapped around her finger. There doesn't seem to be much we can do about it but shut up and smile."

"You could put an illegal substance in her Coke and get her totally out of commission," Blake suggested helpfully. "But I don't do drugs, so I wouldn't really advocate that. Let's see, you could arrange for someone to kidnap her and hold onto her just long enough for the commercial to be shot." She grinned and took a sip of coconut milk. "Don't I have a wonderful imagination?"

Patrick and Mary Ellen exchanged glances. "If you knew Vanessa," Patrick said sadly, "you'd know she was unbeatable. She takes the nasty award hands down."

"And she gets such a kick out of making people miserable," Nancy added. "It's really sick."

"Well, then," Blake said, "you'll just have to be nasty back. It's the only thing that works with people like that. I go to this snooty private school on the Upper East Side, see, and there's this one guy who's always bragging about his parents' country house and their sailboat and their trips to Europe every year. He is out to impress, above all. Well, my gang and I decided to turn the tables on him. Every time he comes up with yet another brilliant credential, we one-up him. He's going to Europe for the summer? Okay, one of us says we're going to Africa to help in the famine program. And the guy just *crumbles*!"

Angie shook her head. "I don't think that would work with Vanessa."

Blake shook a chopstick at her. "You could try."

When they finished dinner, Blake signed her name with a flourish on the credit-card form the waitress had left, and pushed her chair back. "Ready for the grand tour? Soho's really neat at night."

"Thanks, Blake," Mary Ellen nodded, "but we sort of have to get back. Early rehearsal with our coach and then a whole day at the studio. But you've been terrific. And we can't thank you enough for the meal. It was good!"

"Don't sound so surprised," Blake laughed. "Of course it was. Tomorrow I take you for home-style Italian. Unless, of course, your money turns up, in which case you can take me."

Pres couldn't get over her generosity. There was a lot to this girl, and he wished he had the time to get to know her better. On first meeting, she was tough, intense, brash, pretty egocentric. But then, after that, she showed her softer side. She was so different from anyone he'd ever known that he wondered whether his initial attraction was built on curiosity rather than anything else. Of course, she was great-looking, and full of energy and ambition, but she wasn't Claudia. He felt slightly guilty, letting Blake pay for his meal and entertain his friends, when he didn't have any way of reciprocating. And that included emotional giving — not only monetary.

It had grown colder since they'd entered the restaurant, and they all hurried along the street, welcoming the warm blasts of air that came up at them from the subway gratings.

"Now, you take this train back, understand? And get off at Fiftieth Street. Keep your wits about you," Blake instructed them. "I'm going east. See you tomorrow — same time, same station."

"You're not going home alone!" Pres exclaimed.

"Why not? I usually do, unless my date lives nearby." She gave him a soft pat on the back. "Brown belt, remember?"

"Doesn't matter," Pres said, firmly taking her by the arm. "I'm taking you home. I want to," he added, when she started to object.

"Dontcha love it!" Blake giggled, tucking her gloved hand in Pres's pocket. "He's such a gentleman."

"They don't call him that in Tarenton," Angie laughed.

"Well, it's different here," Blake told her. "Everything is. Okay, guys, have a good day — and don't let that Vanessa creature get you down. Something rotten will happen to her if you think positively." She pulled Pres along after her, waving over her head to the others as they disappeared around the corner.

"Boy," Walt exclaimed, as they started down into the subway. "I wish we could sic *her* on Vanessa. Blake looks like she can handle anything — and anyone."

Mary Ellen nodded thoughtfully, then shook

her head. "But can Pres handle *her*? That's the question."

Nobody could answer, because at that moment, a train pulled into the station, and they couldn't even hear themselves think.

CHAPTER

It was seven A.M. when a very tired group of cheerleaders assembled in the deserted ballroom of the hotel. The only people around were the cleaning staff, and the whish of brooms and mops was the accompaniment to the squad's rather desultory warm-up.

"Let's see some energy!" Ardith encouraged them. "I don't care what time it is — and I certainly don't care to hear about your busy evening last night. You are in New York for one purpose, and one purpose only."

"To jump up and down for some dumb soap," Walt complained, falling into a heap at Ardith's feet. "Oh, listen, this routine is so bad. I mean, we could do better. We *have* done better." He pulled himself to his feet and yanked Olivia over to stand in front of him.

"Clean, Clean is bubble, Clean, Clean is pure," he sang, improvising a few steps. He stopped, went back, did it again, and added a turn and a spread-eagle leap. "Now you jump up on me in a thigh stand, Livvy, and Mary Ellen, you get on Pres's shoulders. Like this, see?"

"And then we can do somersaults into splits in a diagonal pattern to the beat," Angie said, showing Nancy what she meant.

"I like that," Olivia nodded. "Maybe for the chorus, we could all do Flying Russians in a circle, and end up with handsprings from the floor." The others tried it and approved.

In the next half hour, the group had created a brand new dance, one that had spirit, and a lot of energy. The thing about it was, it seemed right for them. It had none of the false polish and awkward moves of Dan Moore's choreography, but instead, had a flow and rhythm that only a group that had been working together for a long time could achieve. It was exciting, too. It didn't look like the same old hack stuff on television every day.

"Well," Ardith said when they'd finished, breathless and smiling, "that's all very nice, but what are you going to do with it?"

"Sell it to an advertising company?" Patrick suggested. He had been snapping away throughout their run-through and now, bent down on one knee to get a candid shot of Mary Ellen leaning back to back with Angie. The two of them were perspiring, their blonde hair merging together in careless profusion.

"One thing's for sure," Walt gasped, reaching for the bottle of water he always kept handy, "Clean Soap won't buy it. So, considering that time is money, I guess we should go over what we actually have to do today, right, Mrs. Engborg?"

"That was the general idea I was trying to convey, yes," she smiled softly. "Let's see how much you remember." She marched over to one side to watch them. "Though I must say," she added kindly, "I like your version better."

"That, and a token, will get us on the subway," Nancy laughed.

"If we could *afford* one," Angie said despondently.

"Hey, none of that. We all promised not to panic about the money until we'd checked at the studio," Ardith said firmly. "All right now, from the top. One, and two. . . ."

They rehearsed their parts, and Ardith marked Vanessa's steps in front of them. Nobody had invited Vanessa to their private rehearsal. The truth was that they were hoping she'd come to the studio cold and mess up the whole thing. But, to their amazement, this was not the case. Vanessa was waiting for them when the freight elevator deposited them at HPS Advertising two hours later, and she was all warmed up and ready to work. Today she was wearing a stunning outfit of hot-pink tap pants and a matching pink and gray wrestling T-shirt over a gray leotard. Her dark hair was tied to one side with a pink ribbon.

"Hello, folks!" she called cheerily from her perch up on a sawhorse, facing one of the video machines. Elio, the cameraman, was peering at Vanessa through his lens as she posed one way and then another. "I was just letting Elio test me for my best camera angles."

"The best one is where your back is turned to him," Patrick muttered, getting his own equipment set up.

"The best one is the trick shot where they make you disappear," Walt said softly so that only Olivia and Mary Ellen heard him.

"Well, well, here's our crew!" Harris Scheckner, his wool scarf still wrapped around his skinny neck, came in from the back room, carrying a cup of coffee. A very harried-looking older woman followed him with a sketchbook. She was followed by Casey, who was going over some papers.

"Mr. Scheckner," Angie said, striding up to him and crossing her fingers for luck, "did you or Casey find my makeup case in the dressing room, by any chance?"

"Not me," Casey shrugged. "And I always check out the premises before I leave at night."

"Sorry," Harris said. "But we'll be taking care of your makeup. Just leave everything to us."

Angie bit her lower lip. "It's not that. The problem is, we had all our money — nearly every penny — in that case. I've looked everywhere for it."

"We think Angie's makeup kit was stolen, Mr. Scheckner," Walt told him. "And that leaves us up the creek, in terms of cash, you see. We were wondering — "

"It'll all be taken care of," Harris assured them. "Just tell Casey what you need and she'll write you a check. Now before you get started with Dan this morning," he went on, oblivious to the sighs of relief around him, "I want Linda here, our costume designer, to measure you all for costumes. And then Casey will take you over for your haircuts."

Nancy and Mary Ellen exchanged anxious looks. "Haircuts?" Angie said. "Nobody told us anything about haircuts."

"Well, dear," Vanessa patted her own dark mane, "you can't actually believe they'd put you in front of the cameras without trimming that mess of yours."

Dan bustled into the room in time to hear her last comment. "Didn't you tell them about this, Harris?" the choreographer demanded.

Harris threw up his hands. "Can I remember everything? What do you think I do around here all day?" He turned back to the cheerleaders with an apologetic look on his face. "We're not talking about a trim. We're talking about a look. A major new look."

Walt shrugged and folded his arms. "We have a look already. It's the Tarenton Cheerleading Squad look, Mr. Scheckner."

"Well, of course, that's okay for your little football games and such," Harris smiled. "But for the commercial — " he grabbed the sketchbook from Linda, who had been standing beside him patiently all this time — "now, *this* is a selling look." He displayed the open pages to the group.

Olivia gasped audibly. "You can't be serious. We can't wear those costumes!"

"And we can't have our hair cut that way," Mary Ellen said, a pang of anxiety coursing through her. The drawings showed four skimpily clad girls wearing red and white satin halter-tops with sequinned spaghetti straps and spangles across the chest. The tiny red cheering skirts barely covered the tops of their thighs, and the legs were covered with mesh stockings that led down to white patent leather dance pumps. But the hair was even worse. Each model's head had been shorn drastically, and the short little ends had been teased and sprayed upright. The poor girls looked like they'd stuck their fingers in an electric socket. The renderings of the boys weren't quite as extreme — the hair at least looked normal — but the costumes featured breakaway leg panels that the girls were supposed to tear off during the course of the commercial.

"I don't think this is really us," Mary Ellen said, looking at the drawings again. She had to go to the modeling agency at lunchtime and she was terribly nervous as it was. "Mr. Scheckner, please, couldn't we all just get our ends cut off?" She flipped up a golden blonde lock for his inspection. "There's really nothing wrong with the way we look now."

Dan rubbed his eyes before reaching in his shirt pocket for a cigarette. "Harris, for Pete's sake! I'm not going to stand here arguing with a bunch of kids. I have work to do. So will you please get them measured so we can start the rehearsal? Please?"

Pres stalked over to the man. "Now you listen

87

to me a second. We are not submitting to a total make-over just to do this dumb sixty-second commercial, and that's final."

Harris rushed between them, trying to keep as much distance between Dan and Pres as possible. "Don't worry about a thing, kids. I understand your feelings, but believe me, this is all for the best. When you see yourselves on camera, you're going to thank me."

"Pres, darling," Vanessa smirked, "you're just jealous because you don't get a haircut. I think we'll all look so wonderfully trendy. Won't they eat their hearts out back in Tarenton when they see our New York cuts?" She took a drawing and studied it thoughtfully. "I think I'll look really chic and interesting with short hair."

"Well, Vanessa, any improvement is welcome," Walt grinned. Then he hugged Olivia, who had turned a ghastly shade of gray. "Don't worry, sweetie. I won't let them harm a hair of your pretty head."

"Mr. Scheckner, Mr. Moore," Ardith interjected, "I think you may be making a big mistake here. The Tarenton cheerleaders are known for their distinctive uniforms, and for their different but simple hairstyles. To change all that would be to change them. And the reason you picked them for this commercial is precisely because they are exactly what they seem to be — a group of wholesome, clean-cut kids."

"Oh, honestly!" Dan clapped his hands together to get everyone's attention. "I want to start work now. Linda, take their measurements. Mrs. Engborg, please, if you wouldn't mind, I think it would be better if you didn't attend the rehearsal today — or tomorrow or the next day. You can either sit in the back room or take a walk."

The silence in the room was deafening. Ardith's small, muscular body contracted into a tight ball of contained fury. "Whatever you say," she growled between gritted teeth. "I'll see you kids back at the hotel later." She nodded before turning on her heel and walking abruptly out of the studio. Nobody could believe it — this stupid man, who knew nothing about anything, had just told their coach to leave!

"All right," Harris chimed in. "I want you to give Dan your absolute attention. We have a lot of work to do — we see the client on Monday. You can wait till then to have your haircuts, but after he okays the sketches, you are all going under the ax — or rather, the scissors. No protests or you are out of the number. Got it?"

"Linda," Dan suggested, "take them in there one at a time. Vanessa, honey, let's go over your solo again." He gave the pianist the downbeat and led Vanessa through her steps while the camera followed her around the floor. The lights were hot and bright; the six cheerleaders were hot and bothered.

"This is so awful I can't believe it," Nancy murmured after coming back from her costume fitting.

"I can't have my hair cut," Mary Ellen whimpered. "Not like that. I have to see the people at this agency looking like my pictures. What am I going to do?"

Patrick put an arm around her protectively.

"Just put your foot down. If all of you say you won't do it — "

"They'll throw us out and get some professional dancers who will. And then Harris won't pay us the expense money, and we'll never get out of here," Angie moaned.

"I'd like to see all of you up front — and now," Dan shouted. "The pickup orchestra's coming after lunch, so I want you to be word-and-movement perfect by the time they get here. Places, please."

The squad worked hard — they didn't know how to perform any other way. But in the back of their minds lurked the terror of the finished product. What would they actually look like when these people got through with them? And how would they live with their new image afterward?

"Elio, shoot them from over here. Van, honey, here's your mark, remember? Don't get off your mark. You three, that's right," he said, pointing to Olivia, Walt, and Angie. "Let's get closer to Vanessa on that last bit. I have to shoot you all together."

"Just shoot her, why don't you?" Walt grumbled, doing the step again. "You'll be doing the world a favor."

"I like that!" Dan yelled when Pres lifted Mary Ellen above his chest and then spun her around his head. "Keep it, just like that! But more — give me more!"

"Time, Dan," Casey reminded him at one o'clock.

"Are we excused?" Mary Ellen had been looking at her watch for the past half hour in an increasing frenzy of anticipation. What if he didn't let her go in time for her appointment?

"I think once more will do it," the choreographer said.

"No, Dan," Casey said firmly. "These guys are not going to be paid overtime," she said, pointing to the camera and lighting people. "Which means we break here."

He shrugged, then snapped his fingers to indicate he was finished with the group.

"Can I get my hair cut now, Harris?" Vanessa asked. "I'd really like to have time to live with my new image a bit, you know, before I go national with it."

"Good idea, sweetie. Casey, set her up, will you?" Harris directed as he walked hurriedly out of the studio.

"Oh, can you believe her?" Nancy whispered, as the girls hurried away back to the dressing room. "She was full of herself before, but now, she'll be intolerable. I can't stand it!" She looked at her own lovely brown hair longingly in one of the mirrors. "Good-bye, good looks," she murmured.

"You shouldn't worry," Angie said, sitting heavily beside her. "You and Mary Ellen would look great even if they shaved your heads. I, on the other hand, will look like a bedraggled dandelion with all that stuff sticking up on top."

"I won't do it," Olivia stated emphatically. "It's not me. It's not us."

"Look, you guys, we'll have to worry about this later, okay?" Mary Ellen grabbed her duffle bag and the pictures she'd brought with her and

91

made a mad dash for the front door. "Patrick's taking me to my appointment. Wish me luck!"

She was gone before the others could say a word. As the door slammed behind her, Olivia shook her head sorrowfully. "I hope she won't be as disappointed about the modeling as she's going to be about this commercial. And her hair."

"How could things be any worse?" Nancy looked about as downcast as the other girls had ever seen her. This whole thing had turned into a total and utter disaster.

CHAPTER

"Here! This is the stop! Oh, please, can we get off here?" Mary Ellen thrust her way to the front of the Fifth Avenue bus as Patrick maneuvered his way around the other passengers to follow her.

"Rear door," the driver said, not looking at Mary Ellen. "Push it when the green light goes on."

"But, oh you've missed my stop!" She was sweating now.

"I don't stop at that corner. Here," the driver said, pulling close to the curb. "I stop here. All right, you win. You can get out the front. *This* time," he specified.

She was running as soon as she hit the pavement, looking for the number on the building. She turned to Patrick with a desperate look on her face. "I'm late. They'll refuse to see me. It's all over."

"It's not. Mary Ellen, will you please calm down? This is not a meeting with the President of the United States, you know."

"It's more important than that! Much more. Patrick, this is the beginning of my whole life." She looked at him in frustration, wondering how he could be so placid, so unconcerned. If he didn't know what this appointment meant to her, he clearly didn't understand her at all.

Patrick shrugged, then pulled open the door of the building. "Listen, I just want to tell you — " he began in a soft voice.

"Not now. I can't concentrate. How do I look?" She licked her finger, then ran it over her eyebrows, securing her black portfolio under her arm as she did so. She'd seen a segment of a TV magazine show a couple of months ago about professional models, and she'd learned that the first thing she would need to go out into the field was a portfolio and a set of pictures and resumes to hand out to people. She'd methodically set about collecting every good photo Patrick had ever taken of her and mounting them neatly on construction paper. She had pasted her resume — pretty sparse, but she did manage to fill up one page — on the back of one shot, a smiling rendition of herself wearing her cheerleading uniform, leaping into the air with sheer joy. She'd been so pleased with the results when she first put her book together. It didn't look like an amateur job, not at all.

"You look gorgeous, as usual," Patrick grinned. He felt for her, but he wished she wasn't banking everything on this one interview. It wasn't that he expected her to be disappointed, but he had a feeling that it wouldn't all be totally clear sailing. And he hated to see her hurt.

"Fifth floor, right," Mary Ellen was muttering to herself as she pressed the elevator button. "Oh, I hope I'm what they're looking for." The elevator came to a halt in front of them, and they got in. The door shut slowly, and the numbers began lighting up on the panel above them.

"A kiss for good luck." Patrick smiled, slipping an arm around her shoulders and pressing her to him. But to his amazement, she jerked away.

"You'll ruin my lipstick," she barked. "Oh, please, Patrick, not now!" She was impatient and anxious, and she didn't even notice the angry look on his face. He couldn't stand it when she pulled away from him like that.

"Are you sure I look okay?" She peered at herself in the chrome plate of the elevator number panel, and saw a blurred picture: the wide-set eyes, the pert nose, the perfect mouth, now tight and pursed. Suddenly, she wasn't as sure of herself and her looks as she usually was.

"You look fine," Patrick grumbled as the elevator came to a halt and the doors opened.

Her brows creased as she finally turned to stare at him. "You don't want me to get this, do you?" she asked in a pinched voice.

"What are you talking about?"

"You hope they won't want me. Because if they do, it means my life in Tarenton is a thing of the past. And you can't bear the thought of that." She shook her head, and when he didn't answer, she went on. "I wish you could be happy for me, Patrick."

He took her hand, noticing how damp and clammy it was. "I'll only be happy when I know you're getting all the best. And I'm not sure this is it, that's all." He smiled and unlinked his fingers from hers. She had been clutching onto them as though they were a lifeline back to the safety of her past, of everything she knew. In Tarenton, she was Miss Popularity, captain of the cheerleading team, the prettiest girl in school. Here, she was just an out-of-towner, feeling stranded at sea.

"Hey, lighten up," Patrick encouraged her. "You don't want them to think you're scared."

"I *am* scared. Scared to death," she whispered, falling back a step. The painted letters on the frosted glass door, DANA MODELS, loomed before her.

Patrick smoothed back the hair from her forehead, then moved away from her, giving her a gentle push toward the door. "You're gonna knock 'em dead, kid. What have you got to be scared about? You're more beautiful and more terrific than any fifty New York models. Believe me."

At last, she smiled at him. "You're my best cheering section, you know that?"

He nodded, praying that nothing would happen in the next half hour that would take her away from him once and for all. "I'll always be rooting for you," he said simply.

The door opened and three very tall, exceptionally thin girls — two redheads and a brunette

— came striding out, carrying their sleek black portfolios under their arms. They were dressed casually, in jeans and multicolored leg warmers, and each of them was buried in contrasting layers of T-shirts and bulky sweaters. They were chatting away about a shoot they'd just been assigned in the Caribbean, and the new health club they'd just joined, and they sounded completely and utterly professional.

Mary Ellen paused and took a deep breath. She was painfully aware of her clothing, of the fact that in her navy wool slacks and her beige cotton blouse with its ascot tie, she looked like a schoolgirl, not a model. How could she have been so dumb as to dress as though she were on her way to a college interview?

"Yes, may I help you?" The receptionist looked at Mary Ellen and Patrick over the tops of her half-glasses, and then glanced back down at her blinking telephone. "Just a second, please." She took the call, then looked up again. "You two are here to see. . . ?"

"Ah, it's just her," Patrick said quickly, jerking a thumb in Mary Ellen's direction. "I'm here for moral support only." He smiled, but the receptionist didn't seem at all interested.

Mary Ellen cleared her throat. "I have an appointment with Mary Ellen Kirkwood. I mean," she said, laughing nervously, *"I'm* Mary Ellen. I have an appointment with Evelyn at one-thirty."

"Out to lunch right now. Have a seat, why don't you?" The receptionist waved them over to the bank of orange vinyl seats and went back to her telephones.

During the next fifteen minutes, a lot of people came and went. Every time somebody walked in the front door, Mary Ellen would rearrange her position, trying to look more sophisticated and bright-eyed. Each time, she would look hopefully at the newcomer. Nobody ever glanced at her.

"Now we're going to be late getting back to rehearsal. This is turning out to be a real bummer of a day," Mary Ellen sighed as the door opened again to admit a messenger from the corner coffee shop carrying three lunch bags.

A tiny, squat woman emerged from the back room. "Oh, hello. You're my one-thirty, aren't you? I'm Evelyn. Sorry to keep you waiting, dear."

Mary Ellen was slightly annoyed. The woman must have been there all the time. She stood, remembering to keep her back very straight, and walked toward Evelyn with her hand outstretched, turning on that glowing smile that never failed to get a reaction. She no longer even remembered that Patrick was right behind her.

"Come on, this way." Evelyn paid no attention to the sparkling smile. "Could I have your resume, please?" She reached a hand in back of her as she plowed her way down the corridor and Mary Ellen tried to keep up.

"Yes, well, I brought all my pictures and I thought I'd — "

"Look, sweetie, just your resume right now. I want to see what you've done." Evelyn led her inside a small office, overflowing with contact sheets and glossy head shots of beautiful girls. Just a glance at the few scattered on the desk made Mary Ellen's heart pound harder. Back home, she'd never had any idea the competition would be so fierce.

"I did write down my experience," she said in a meek voice. "I model regularly at Marnie's — that's a boutique in the Pineland Mall. And right now, I'm in New York with my cheerleading squad, filming a commercial for Clean Soap."

"No professional jobs, though?" Evelyn quickly flipped the pages of Mary Ellen's book, barely glancing at the pictures. She leaned over to make a note on the pad in front of her, then turned the book back to the nervous girl seated across the table from her.

"Well, the commercial is. It's going to be national, and — "

Evelyn's phone was ringing. "I'm afraid we don't start off amateurs here. Some agencies do, but we don't. It was nice to meet you, though. Good luck." She answered the phone and turned away.

This couldn't be happening! It couldn't be completely over so fast, without any hope or promise at all. The woman hadn't even given her a chance. But Mary Ellen was nothing if not ambitious. She had never been able to let opportunities fly by her without at least making an effort. She sat, trying not to look miserable, until the phone call was over.

"Uh, I was thinking," she said as soon as Evelyn hung up. "Since I'm in New York right now, maybe I could take over for one of your regular runway girls in the garment district. Just for an hour or so. I wouldn't expect to get paid," she added hastily, "but that way you could see what I can do."

Evelyn gave her a curious look, as though she hadn't expected Mary Ellen to still be there when she got off the phone. A hundred girls a week walked into her office from Way Out There, USA, and she invariably sent them away. For some reason, though, she saw something a little different in this one.

"Not possible. Everybody's booked up a month in advance. I can't bump a model." She frowned, then examined Mary Ellen carefully. "Would you stand up a second? How tall are you?" She glanced down at the stats on Mary Ellen's resume.

"Five eight. And I weigh one twenty-five."

"All right. Not bad for runway, but you'd be too hefty for magazines. I don't know. . . ." She leaned back in her chair. "Stand up a sec."

Mary Ellen jumped to attention.

Evelyn laughed. "Not so stiff. You're not a candidate for basic training. Walk across the room, why don't you?"

Mary Ellen walked.

"Um. Turn. Yes, fine. Look up. Now look this way. Turn your head. Okay. Head down, eyes up. No, no, the other way!" Evelyn kept the instructions coming in rapid-fire succession until Mary Ellen felt dizzy.

"Yes. Well, you're green, I'll say that for you. Not bad-looking, although we have a lot of your type. Let me see your hands." She walked up to Mary Ellen and critically scrutinized first her right, then her left hand. "Yes, these are good. Nice long fingers, well-rounded nails. Maybe we

100

could get you some hand modeling. We've got a dish-detergent thing coming up at the end of next week."

Mary Ellen wanted to cry. All this excitement, this anticipation, just to be told that she had long fingers. Wouldn't Vanessa cackle with glee if she heard that Mary Ellen's big chance had ended up underwater with the dirty dishes.

"Oh, I have to go home on Wednesday. We have to be back at school, and there's a game next Saturday night."

Evelyn shrugged, looking right through her again. "Of course. Well, if you're ever in the city again, give me a call and we'll see what we can do. And now, I'm afraid my next appointment is here. It's been good meeting you." She went back to her desk and closed Mary Ellen's book, then handed it to her with her picture and resume on top.

"Oh, please, keep those. I brought them for you," Mary Ellen said hastily, thrusting her credentials back at the woman.

Evelyn smiled at her. "Dear, I have so many of these things lying around. It would just end up in the circular file." She pointed to the wastebasket. "But as I said, if you're ever in town. . . ." She let the sentence trail off and started to dial. Mary Ellen knew she'd been dismissed.

"Right. Thanks." She turned toward the door, stiffly straightening her back. It was stupid to slink out like a beaten dog, but it was hard to keep her chin high all the way back to the reception area.

Patrick looked up from his magazine as he

saw her coming down the hall. He scanned her face, then stood up. "I don't think I have to ask how it went."

"Don't," was all she said.

They took the elevator back down and walked outside. Life was going on, the city bustling just as it had an hour ago, and yet Mary Ellen felt like she was in a time warp where everything had stopped dead around her.

Patrick steered her across Fifth Avenue with a firm hand. Mary Ellen was such a strange mixture. Here she was, a ball of fire, a girl who was out to whip the world. Yet sometimes, she was so vulnerable, so lost. Maybe that was the part of her he loved best. "We're a little late," he told her as they got to the other side. "I've been saving this lonely five-dollar bill of mine for something special, so why don't we grab a cab back to the studio?" he suggested quietly.

"What? Yeah, sure. Good idea." It wasn't that she felt rotten, actually. It was like she didn't feel anything at all — and that was worse.

"Mary Ellen?" He nudged her gently, trying to get some reaction out of her. When he got none, he sighed, then raised his hand to hail the taxi that was barreling down the street toward them. It stopped within inches of the couple, and Patrick pulled the door open.

"It was only one agency," he reminded her after giving the driver the address of the studio. "Only one interview."

She shook her head. "I don't want to discuss it." She didn't need logic right now. If she jumped at that bright star she so desperately wanted, and she tripped, Patrick was always going to be waiting to catch her with open arms. It was usually comforting to know that if she failed as a New York model, she could come home to the one who loved her. But wouldn't that be running away from something rather than running toward it? She felt so mixed up right now, so terribly hurt.

"I understand." He sat back, watching the street numbers flash by. This city was so big, so cruel to so many. It was exciting and exhilarating and all the things they wrote about in the guide books, but it could also be a pretty lousy place. One thing was sure — Patrick Henley had been out of Tarenton a whopping three days, and he was homesick for it already. He only wished that the wonderful girl beside him could feel the same.

They were, thankfully, only a little late, and no one really noticed when they walked in and Mary Ellen raced to the dressing room to change. Patrick watched her disappear behind the door, and then he walked over to the piano where he'd left his camera before the lunch break. A small group of musicians was tuning up, and the other cheerleaders were lying around on the floor, stretching or relaxing.

"How'd she do?" Olivia whispered as Dan clapped his hands to get everyone's attention.

"Is Mary Ellen going to be on the cover of *Seventeen* next month?" Nancy demanded.

Patrick's downcast eyes spoke for him. He didn't have to say a word.

"I thought she seemed upset when she went in there," Angie said. "Oh, dear."

"She's going to be more upset after she sees Vanessa with her haircut, I bet," Pres predicted.

"How bad is it?" Patrick asked.

"Who knows?" Walt shook his head. "They were just about to unveil her when you walked in."

And then the dressing room door opened. Mary Ellen walked out first, in a state of total shock. Vanessa was right behind her, and she was clutching what was left of her hair with both hands, as if to reassure herself that there was still something up there. She looked as though they had stuck her head in a blender.

"There's our beauty!" Harris beamed as he saw her. "The minute I saw you back in your little hometown, I knew there was a fashion plate inside, yearning to burst out." He came over and fluffed the jagged ends of Vanessa's new coiffure. "Isn't it *you*, darling? Isn't it the real you?"

"It's awful!" Vanessa screeched, dissolving into tears. "It'll take forever to grow it out. Oh, how could you have done this to me?"

Walt crossed his arms, thoughtfully examining Vanessa's head. "It couldn't have happened to a nicer person," he said.

And then they all cracked up. All the hostility they'd ever felt toward Vanessa exploded in great gales of laughter. Mary Ellen couldn't feel sorry for herself now, not when she saw the way Vanessa looked. Nancy, Angie, and Olivia started giggling, and the giggles gradually built and expanded until they were full-fledged guffaws. Pres and Patrick were practically rolling on the floor, and Walt was doubled over, the tears streaming down his cheeks. Even the musicians were chortling. Vanessa's crying stopped abruptly as her face grew red with fury. She was the star of the commercial, wasn't she? And this was the way she was supposed to look. What the rest of them thought didn't count.

"On Monday, you'll look like this, too, girls," Dan said calmly, when the frenzied laughter had worn itself out. "You all have to match, you know."

There was shocked silence from the cheerleaders. How were they ever going to get out of this mess?

"Back to work, folks," Dan announced. "Peaches, what about a downbeat?" He smiled over at Harris as the orchestrated strains of the soap jingle filled the large studio. Vanessa took her place at the center, smiling as best she could at the camera in front of her.

"We aren't going to let this happen, are we?" Nancy whispered to the others as she lined up between Olivia and Angie.

"Never," Olivia said staunchly.

"Over my dead body," Mary Ellen said, pulling herself together. She might be a failure as a model, she might be back in the chorus line instead of up front where she deserved to be, but one thing was certain — she still had her pride. And she had her friends around her. With those two assets, what more did she really need?

CHAPTER

"I don't really feel like going out," Angie sighed.

"Me, either," Olivia said, staring out the hotel window at the sunny Sunday morning. "And it's not fair to Blake for us to mooch off her every time we see her."

"Oh, come on, girls. This is our chance to really see New York, do the town," Pres encouraged them. He was looking forward to seeing Blake again, even though he felt vaguely as though he was two-timing Claudia. Of course, he'd done nothing to feel guilty about, and Blake was just an acquaintance, eager to show him and his friends a good time. But should he even be having a good time?

Last night, late, he'd called California, trying to get some information about Claudia, but the hospital wouldn't put him through to her, and none of her family was around. He'd been panicky, upset, guilty that here he was, having a fine time while the girl he loved was. . . . Well, where and how was she, exactly? If he only knew. Yet he was perfectly able to set aside his concerns and enjoy being with Blake. Was there something wrong with him? Was he just a cold-hearted monster who lived for the moment? Or was it just that, right now, with so much on his mind, he needed something lighthearted and carefree? He hoped it was the latter.

The girls couldn't seem to make up their minds about the day, either, but their problem was nothing like Pres's. "I don't think I'd be such wonderful company today," Nancy sighed.

"I'd drag you all down," Angie agreed. "You guys go on without us."

"Might as well go out and party now, before your haircuts, while you still all look good," Walt joked. "You know, the condemned women ate a hearty meal."

"Not funny." Olivia scowled at him.

The phone beside one of the beds buzzed softly and Pres dove for it. "Hi. Hi, Blake! We'll be right there," he told her. He set down the receiver and looked at the others. "Well?"

The girls all looked glum; the boys seemed slightly more together. "I say we go and actually try to enjoy ourselves," Patrick suggested. "Hey, how bad can it be?"

The seven of them found Blake waiting for them at the elevator bank. Today she was wearing a terrific cream-colored jogging suit under her red cape with little red Robin Hood boots that matched perfectly. "Ready?" she asked, grinning.

107

Then she saw their faces. "Whew, do you people look awful! Like you were just told you were grounded for a month, or something. You still worrying about that money? Or is it your nemesis, Vanessa?"

"It's a lot of things," Pres told her. "But we're willing to let you try to cheer us up."

"I guess I have my work cut out for me, huh?"

"I don't know," Nancy sighed. "Maybe it's useless. Maybe New York is just too much for hicks like us."

Blake frowned at her. "How can you say that? The most wonderful city in the world and you want to give up on it? Listen, that's the point of it. New York isn't easy, it's not like a pleasant ride in the country. It's a challenge — but it's the best challenge," she said proudly. "It's an absolutely gorgeous, wonderful, marvelous, special place. And I won't let you suggest it's anything else!" she went on expansively. "I want you to see everything, all of it. And you have to see it the right way, which is walking. Taxis and buses are for tourists. Okay, I want to see chins up, campers! I want to see smiles on those cheerleading faces. Isn't that what you guys are known for? Smiles on your faces no matter what your real attitude is?"

Mary Ellen gave her a skeptical look. "I think you've read too much propaganda about people like us. Cheerleaders aren't necessarily cheery by nature."

"Well, do it for me. Please?" Blake was teasing, but she seemed to understand that they needed her gentle prodding, so she didn't let up.

"All right, we're on our way. First stop, the Plaza Fountain."

Blake walked their feet off. They tooled up Broadway, then cut over on Central Park South. People were out in droves, dressed in casual Sunday attire. A man with a gaily colored parrot on his shoulder passed by; the parrot said good morning and told them it was thirty-eight degrees outside. The cheerleaders, after only a moment's pause, thanked the parrot.

"See what I mean?" Blake gushed. "Only in New York, right? There — there's the fountain. This is history, folks. F. Scott Fitzgerald himself cavorted around it, not to mention yours truly." She put out her hand to Pres and dragged him to the fountain. Its carved stone figures and wide gray basin were beautiful, even inspiring.

A mime, wearing white-face and a black top hat, was working the crowd around the fountain, following people and imitating their gestures and expressions. The kids watched him for a while, then found that they themselves were the objects of his interest.

Angie found her spirits lighter. She wandered away from the group, her mood one hundred percent better, and went to stare at the fountain. For the first time since she'd been in this city, she found something really beautiful to admire in it. "What a lovely place," she exclaimed, putting out her hands to the others. Mary Ellen and Pres joined her, doing a little dance around the circumference of the fountain, as Blake looked on in amusement.

"Wow, you can dress 'em up, but they still act

like they're from Tarenton," she quipped. "Anybody interested in the Empire State Building? Or would you rather see Trump Tower?"

"I want to see everything," Mary Ellen stated firmly.

"Well, we'll try our utmost," Blake sighed, looking at her watch. "But it really would take weeks. You'll just have to come back."

Mary Ellen nodded solemnly and Patrick instinctively moved closer. He saw the wistful look in her eyes, and for a moment, he thought he saw something like envy. If Mary Ellen could have traded places with Blake Norton for a while, would she have done it? Or did she know herself well enough to see that she was nothing like street-smart Blake, and that she really wouldn't be happy if she stayed here?

The next stop was Rockefeller Center, where they stood and watched the skaters spinning gracefully beneath the shadow of Atlas, holding up the world.

"What about Forty-second Street?" Walt demanded. "Can we go there next?"

"You're kidding!" Blake made a face. They looked at her expectantly. "You're not kidding. Well, it's ugly as sin, but if you insist. . . ." She shrugged, then led them on downtown, passing the X-rated movie theaters and souvenir shops with a disgusted smirk. "Why people think of this as the hub of New York is beyond me," she told them. "Not worth the trip. Onward. Empire State Building is next."

Everyone was dizzy and hungry by noon, but Blake refused to give them a break. "We don't have much time, and we have all of downtown to do."

"This is harder than a whole day of rehearsal," Olivia grumbled. "Not that I would have missed it," she added with a smile.

Blake turned to her knowingly. "So you don't think New York is such a terrible place anymore?"

"Terrible?" Angie was glowing. "It's great!"

"See what I mean?" Blake giggled. "It just takes a little time to fall in love with it, is all. Okay, now for something completely different. We can have brunch at some glassed-in fern place up here, or dim sum in Chinatown, or pasta in Little Italy, or maybe a ride on the Staten Island ferry. What'll it be?"

"A ferry, in this weather?" Nancy asked skeptically.

"It's the best," Blake promised her. "Unless one of you guys is prone to seasickness."

Nobody was, so Blake allowed them to get on a subway and ride to South Ferry, conceding that this much walking combined with what she had in mind for them later might just do them in. The ferry was just pulling out as they approached it, and they broke into a run, dashing through the entrance gate, laughing, happy for the first time in days. There was a sense of exhilaration among them as the whistle blew, and they followed Blake up to the top deck, pulling their hats down and their collars up. The misty scent of the bay sharpened their senses, made them aware of yet another facet of this amazing city.

"Look, there's Wall Street," Blake pointed,

raising her voice above the slap of the waves against the big old boat. "And up there is South Street Seaport. You can't really see from here, but farther north is where the *Intrepid* is docked, and . . . well, there's too much," she laughed, putting her arm through Pres's. "Just ask if you want to know the local landmarks."

They rode the ferry back and forth twice, marveling at the incredible views of the city spread out before them, the haze of the sky above muddy green waters. Finally, cold and starving, they docked and made directly for Little Italy via Chinatown. The crowded streets were unlike anything else they had seen of New York so far, like a set from a movie in a foreign locale. The smells of unusual spices, the stands of fruits and vegetables that none of them could recognize, the intense haggling in a guttural language, added a feeling of mystery to this part of their trip. And then, as suddenly as they had entered the world of the exotic East, within one block, they were serenaded by the sweet strains of an Italian melody, and they could almost taste the heady aroma of tomato and freshly baked bread that pervaded the air.

"This is absolutely incredible!" Walt stopped in front of a cozy-looking restaurant that boasted a huge copper espresso machine in the window. Waiters with long white aprons scurried around the room, serving tiny cups of the strong coffee to impatient customers.

"Come on, a nice cappuccíno and a plate of pasta should fix you guys up for the evening. Unless you'd rather have a pizza."

Angie shrugged. "Well, we have it all the time at Pizza Pete's in the mall, but I guess you can never have too much pizza."

"Ah, my dear," Blake said, ushering them through the door and over to a large corner table. "Your pizza place undoubtedly gives you frozen hunks of bread with canned tomato sauce on top. Whereas *this* place makes ambrosia — with mushrooms, artichokes, pepperoni, whatever — in their own fiery brick ovens, imported direct from Naples. Believe me, if what passes for pizza in Tarenton is anything like this, I'll eat a football." She proceeded to wave the waiter over and order for them all.

"You certainly know your way around this city," Pres commented as they sat back, comfortably chewing breadsticks.

"Naturally." Blake was clearly pleased that he'd noticed. And about twenty minutes later, when she saw the pizza coming toward their table, she could almost see their mouths watering. The waiter bore it to them on a platter over his head with obvious pride, as though he'd made it himself.

"Oh, please!" Olivia waved her hands in desperation. "I can't. I'll never be able to do a single cartwheel tomorrow." Then she dug into the pizza, and her face suddenly changed. "This sure isn't like anything I've ever had."

"Now, when we leave here there's a punk club in the East Village that you have to see," Blake exclaimed. "You can't go home and tell your friends you haven't visited the most *in* night spot in all of New York!"

"Easily," Angie said. "I'm beat, Blake. Thanks for the offer, but I have to pass."

"And I was sort of thinking about calling Ben tonight," Nancy confided. She wasn't exactly surprised that, after only a few days, she missed him a lot.

"Right," Blake nodded, seemingly untouched by their protests. "Well, that's cool. If you don't want to come, I'll go by myself. I've been looking forward to this all day."

"You mean," Mary Ellen ventured, "you'd go out to a club all alone? Wouldn't your parents mind? I mean, isn't that sort of dangerous?"

Blake gave her a sly wink. "I love living dangerously, kid. It's the only way." She grinned when Pres shook his head. "It's true. Remember, I told you I know karate."

"Still and all," Pres said softly, "there might be some people who'd care what happened to you."

Blake made a face and shrugged. "My parents don't pay much attention to me."

Walt nodded, feeling a sudden kinship with this very sophisticated, but clearly very lonely, girl. "That's tough."

"Hey, no skin off my nose. I like being on my own."

Patrick and Mary Ellen exchanged a look. It was so easy to see through Blake right now, she might as well have been a pane of glass. They all, on occasion, put up a brave front, and they understood exactly how it felt to be smiling on the outside but miserable inside. "I vote we go," Patrick said firmly. "Let's throw out all schedules and just live it up. I mean, how many times do we get a complete, personalized tour of New York?"

"I agree," Walt said. Olivia agreed, too. Then everyone else chimed in. Blake couldn't have looked happier.

The club was on East Third Street, and no one but a frequent visitor would have known it was there, except for the muffled, dull thud of a backbeat that could have penetrated steel walls. As they walked through the door, the noise level grew steadily until it was a deafening roar that reverberated in their chests.

"This is neat," Pres breathed, looking around. The former storefront had been converted into a kind of cave, with pockets of red light glaring ominously at the dancers who threw themselves carelessly around the postage-stamp-sized floor. There were people wearing only cut-offs and T-shirts, and others in strange costumes. There were people with massive quantities of hair in an assortment of colors and some with hardly any hair at all. Looking at a man with a shaved head and one dangling feather earring, Nancy instinctively reached up to touch her own hair. Was it really going to be cut off in the morning?

"I kind of like it here," Blake agreed, dragging Pres off to dance. "It has a charm all its own."

Walt, Olivia, and Mary Ellen stood by the sidelines, staring, and Patrick, Angie, and Nancy went to the little bar that served only soft drinks. The disc jockey's patter cut into the music, but nobody could understand what he was saying anyway. Flashing videos were running on the walls, ceiling, and floor. People were posing like robots, then moving jerkily to the music. The effect was chaos.

Everyone threw themselves into the spirit of the place. Patrick danced with Angie and Nancy; Walt made it a threesome with Olivia and Mary Ellen; and then, after half an hour and buckets of perspiration, they all switched. Half an hour after that, they forcibly had to yank Blake and Pres off the floor and stick cans of Coke into their hands.

"Only in New York, right?" Blake grinned, her face gleaming with the sweat of her exertions.

"Absolutely," Angie gasped, wiping her neck and forehead. "I can't go on, though. Really, I have to get some rest."

"That's it for us, too," Walt said, moving Olivia aside to make way for three dancers, who were hopping and leaping around, paying very little attention to bystanders. "Do you mind if we skip out?"

"Hey, I've got school tomorrow myself," Blake grinned. "Let's call it a night."

Mary Ellen leaned over and took their guide by both hands. "We can't thank you enough," she said loudly, over the blare of the music. "We never would have seen half of what we got to today if it hadn't been for you."

"Aw, shucks," Blake blushed, leading them out into the street. "My pleasure. I couldn't stand to have you go back to Tarenton without knowing the real New York. You know how to get back to the hotel from here?" They reached the avenue and crossed over. It was late (or early)

116

— after two — and yet there were still people out on the streets. A taxi passed and slowed for them, and Blake waved it down, shoving some money into Pres's hand. "Go on," she urged them.

Pres handed the bills to Patrick, then moved a little closer to Blake. "We'll take the next cab. See you in the A.M., guys," he said to his friends, who piled into the car, too exhausted to say anything but good-night.

In the glow of the streetlights, Pres could see that Blake was just as tired as he was. "I'd suggest a moonlight stroll," he said, smiling, "but I think we both might just keel over before we'd gone a block."

"Guess you're right," she nodded gamely, raising her hand to hail another cab. "It's been super, though. I'm really glad I met you guys."

"So am I." A taxidriver jammed on his brakes in front of the couple, and they hauled themselves inside, collapsing on the seat. Blake let her head rest comfortably on Pres's shoulder.

They sat together, their eyes closed, and for a while, Pres thought she had fallen asleep. But then she stirred and said, "Good thing you're going to be leaving soon."

"Well, that's a nice thing to say!" Pres grumbled.

"I just mean, I'd be the laughing stock of school if anyone thought I'd fallen for a hick."

He caught a glimpse of her face in the light of the streetlamps. She was trying to joke, but there was something very serious about her tone. "And I'd be drummed out of the cheerleaders if you

117

ruined my ladykiller image. *You* picked *me* up, remember?"

She turned up her mouth to him, asking to be kissed. An image of Claudia superimposed itself on Blake's face, and Pres found himself, for once, at a loss. What was he supposed to do? How was he supposed to feel? It would be easy to fall under this girl's spell, to follow wherever she let her lead. But something in him wanted to put on the brakes. He turned her face gently and gave her a peck on the cheek.

"That's all I get?" she complained. "No passion, no declarations of love?" Her tone was flippant now, because she sensed his distance.

"I'm too beat to think clearly. No telling what I'd do," he explained clumsily. "And also, Blake . . . I really like you, you know that."

"But I'm not your type," she shrugged, straightening up. "I know, it's okay," she assured him, moving away from him on the seat. "Driver, next canopy down. Number 119." She stretched and yawned, then wrapped her cape around her. "Call before you leave town, understand?" she told him directly. "Otherwise, I'll get *mean*." She grinned and opened the door as the cab came to a halt.

"I'll talk to you tomorrow," Pres promised, but she was gone already, walking away as easily as could be.

He sat back as the taxi moved on toward his hotel, wondering what all this meant. He knew Blake cared more than she let on, and in a way, he did, too. He'd really believed that when Claudia entered his life, everything he ever felt

118

about girls would change for good, that he would never want anyone else. And yet, he really liked Blake — *more* than liked her, as a matter of fact.

He sighed to himself as the cab pulled up in front of his hotel. If only relationships weren't so complicated, so full of twists and turns and gray areas. Maybe in the morning, things would look clearer. He doubted it, but he could still hope, right? In New York, anything was possible.

CHAPTER

The costumes were ready and waiting when the cheerleaders arrived at rehearsal early Monday morning. Each ridiculous outfit sat on its hanger with the wearer's name tagged to it.

The girls dressed quickly, then walked to the mirrors very, very slowly.

"Oh, no, I can't be seen in public like this!" Angie-moaned. "My mother will kill me."

"This has to be the ugliest creation in the history of the world." Mary Ellen turned to look at the back, then swung around to the front again. "It's trashy."

"I think it looks perfect," Vanessa smirked, combing as best she could the hair she had left. "Your problem, dearheart, is that you don't think you're getting equal time on camera. And whose fault is that?" she grinned. "Certainly not mine."

"Certainly not, Van," Nancy said. She stood

up and matter-of-factly bent over to touch her toes. "You wouldn't have done anything at all to ruin our chances as a group. It was Harris and Dan who decided you fit their concept better than we did. Why, I'm sure if we showed those guys our own version of their jingle, they'd laugh us out of the room."

"Your own version?" Vanessa suddenly looked very suspicious. What was more, she looked worried.

"Yeah, we worked up a little something the other day when we had nothing better to do," Olivia explained, tugging at her tiny skirt to get it a millimeter lower. "Something for just the six of us. Not that it matters," she added.

"Mrs. Engborg is bringing over our Tarenton uniforms today, right?" Olivia came over and stood in front of Vanessa, excluding her from the conversation. "Patrick wants to get those yearbook shots in front of the Clean Soap set. I suppose it's not strictly truthful to take our pictures in our real clothes, but we wouldn't want *this* printed in the yearbook." She looked at herself in dismay, and then shut her eyes tight. Maybe, if she thought about it hard enough, the costume would go away.

"Right." Mary Ellen nodded, drawing a brush through her hair one last time. "At least our classmates will think we looked half decent. That is, until they see us on television." She shuddered, then went on. "Ardith said she'd be over with the uniforms about noon. Boy, does she ever look depressed these days," she added softly.

"It'll do her a world of good to get home

121

again," Angie said. "I think that goes for all of us."

"Not me," Vanessa grinned, bending over to do a few perfunctory stretches. "This is my kind of town." She adjusted the tiny straps on her costume, then went to the door. "I can't wait to show my mother how I look." She walked out, leaving the four girls sitting glumly together.

"I can't believe Mrs. Barlow will approve," Nancy said, shaking her head.

"She won't, but Vanessa has her mother under her thumb. Whatever her darling little baby wants, she gets," Angie sighed.

"I can't believe that Vanessa was ever a darling little baby," Olivia sighed, getting up to do a couple of backbends.

"She wasn't even a baby," Mary Ellen said definitively. "I think she must have hatched, like a vulture."

"Time, kids!" Casey called from the studio. "Mr. Danziger just walked in and he wants to see you."

Mr. Danziger didn't just represent Clean Soap; he *was* Clean Soap. He had inherited the company from his father, who had built it up from a tiny business owned by his grandfather. Now, of course, it was a multimillion-dollar company. Harris had explained to them that no one was to say a word when Mr. Danziger put in his two cents — which he undoubtedly would. Whatever he said, went.

The boys were waiting for them by the piano, limbering up and practicing their steps. When they saw the girls, they blinked a couple of times.

Patrick loped over and put an arm around Mary Ellen's shoulder. "It's not as bad as you think," he whispered.

"How bad *is* it?" She was begging for an honest opinion.

Patrick never failed her. "It's cheap and tawdry, but it's not as bad as you think," he answered promptly.

"Well, will you look at that!" Walt let out a wolf whistle and came over to examine Olivia more closely.

"You don't look so great yourself," she hissed, clucking over his tight pants and the spangled T-shirt that clung to his muscular frame like moss to a tree.

"Kids! This is marvelous. You are the living personification of Clean Soap!" Harris was gushing as he sped across the room, peering at them through his dark glasses. "If I ever had any doubts about the concept — which I didn't, of course — you have just erased them. Mr. Danziger, I'd like to introduce to you the stars of our show: the Tarenton cheering team. And this is our leading lady, Vanessa Barlow," he added when she had wormed her way in front of the other six.

Mr. Danziger was a balding barrel of a man, very tall and very round. His moustache twitched nervously above his thin lips, and there was a deep crease between his brows. He looked like a man who didn't sleep well at night.

"All right, Harris. Let's see what you've got to offer," he said, scowling. Then, shaking his head, he took a seat between Dan Moore and Mrs. Barlow on one side of the room.

"Everybody, this is a take! Let's have some light!" Harris went into action, getting Casey to cue lights, music, and cameras. He brought the group into one corner and got them into a huddle. "Now, give it your all. I want to see smiles wider than the Atlantic Ocean. I want spirit and enthusiasm. I want you to sell this product! Does everyone understand?"

"We won't let you down, Harris," Vanessa said, smiling eagerly. "At least, *I* won't." She waved to her mother, then gave the cheerleaders a disparaging look.

"We'll try to live up to our potential, Mr. Scheckner," Walt said, grinning, but wanting to kick Vanessa in the shins.

"This is a take!" Harris called out, waving his hands in the air. "Roll 'em."

They got into position just as the door opened once more. It was Ardith, carrying an armful of uniforms. She couldn't conceal the look of shock on her face as she beheld her charges totally transformed. She didn't say a word, but nodded to the others and took a seat beside Dan. Harris pointed at Peaches, who gave the cheerleaders the downbeat.

It was all over in sixty seconds. Then, the room was silent, except for the sound of the performers, breathing hard from the exertion of their routine. Mr. Danziger cleared his throat.

"This it it?" he asked.

"Just as promised." Harris folded his arms and tilted his chair back. "We've given you a total concept for your product, Mr. Danziger, something that's going to make sales jump off the charts."

"The only thing this demonstration makes jumpy," Mr. Danziger scowled, "is my heart rate." He stood, drawing himself up to his full height. "Harris Scheckner, you should be ashamed!" he stated.

"But . . . but Mr. Danziger — "

"We have to polish it a little more, of course," Dan explained hastily when he saw the client's face getting progressively redder.

"What do you think you're doing here?" Mr. Danziger was more confused than furious, but the tone of annoyance in his voice was palpable. "You think you are selling sexy cars, or maybe perfume? No, you are *not*." His voice was getting louder. "You are supposed to be selling my soap. *Clean* Soap." He stalked over to the cheerleaders, squinting at Vanessa. "All wrong. This ugly dress, the hair, the movements — it's *all wrong!*"

"Wrong?" Dan Moore couldn't seem to get it through his head that the client wasn't pleased. "But we showed you the specs for the costumes. We told you what we had planned."

"Plans change. Opinions change," Mr. Danziger said stolidly. "Clean Soap does not change."

Harris cleared his throat, then rubbed his hands over his face. "If it's a question of a little revision here and there, I'm sure we can manage that. You see, this routine is still kind of rough, and — "

"Rough! It's wrong. How many times do I have to tell you?" Mr. Danziger walked to the door, grabbing the knob with a hostile grunt. "You've lost the account, Scheckner," he told the man without turning around. "I'm going to another agency."

"Oh, no. Oh, I can't believe this!" Harris was clutching his stomach. The bottom had just fallen out of his entire week.

"Sir? Excuse me, I wonder if I might say something." Mary Ellen had been listening to the argument with a growing sense that she knew exactly what she had to do. As captain of the cheerleaders, it was up to her to speak, even if she got her head handed to her.

"What?" Mr. Danziger turned around, fuming.

"We may have a solution to your problem, sir," she said quietly. "As it happens, we have another version of your jingle ready to show you." She turned on all the lights behind her smile and tossed her blonde hair becomingly. "I have a feeling you may like it better than what you just saw."

"I don't know. . . ." Mr. Danziger was not in a mood to be convinced.

"It'll only take a minute, Mr. Danziger," Walt said cheerily. "Just sit down while we all change our clothes." He winked at Ardith as he went to her to retrieve their uniforms. Their coach was beaming but trying to control herself.

"What's this all about?" Mr. Danziger demanded of Harris, reluctantly wandering back to his seat.

"I, uh . . . well, we'll just have to see, won't we?" Harris was totally baffled, but he wasn't giving anything away. He'd probably lost the account already, so anything that happened now didn't matter very much. Still, it would be stupid to acknowledge to his client that he didn't know what was going on.

The cheerleaders ran into the dressing rooms, tearing off their awful costumes and quickly dressing in their beloved Tarenton red and white. The pleated skirts had been pressed at the hotel, and they stood out becomingly under the white sweaters. The red "T" that announced the group's allegiance had never seemed more appropriate. Today, it stood for "Triumph."

"But what about me?" Vanessa whined, sitting down heavily in front of one of the mirrors.

"Gee, Van," Nancy shrugged, "guess you're out of the picture. It's really a shame you got your hair cut. If you looked anywhere near normal, we might have been able to squeeze you in, but as it is, you'd stick out like a sore thumb."

"Sorry," Olivia said, smirking. "Better luck next time."

"Let's go, kids!" Angie was champing at the bit. "Before this man escapes."

Pres and Walt stood tall as the girls joined them next to the piano. "We need a couple more bars here," Walt said, indicating the place on the sheet music to Peaches, "because we're going to be doing some pretty fancy stuff. Just watch me, okay?"

"Whatever you say, chum," the pianist shrugged.

"And one, and two . . ." Mary Ellen called out.

"Clean, clean is bubble,
Clean, clean is pure.
Won't give your skin trouble,
That's for sure."

The six of them had never worked so well together. The pikes were clean and well-executed, the lifts as high as they had ever been. Olivia leaped proudly from a flying somersault into Walt's outstretched arms with hardly an intake of breath, and Nancy vaulted up to Pres's shoulders as though it were nothing at all. Their voices were loud and clear, and their smiles were genuine. At last, they were doing what they knew how to do — performing something they wholeheartedly believed in.

They came to a rousing finish, Angie and Mary Ellen in splits with their arms raised high above their heads, Olivia and Nancy behind them in parallel flying fishes in Walt's and Pres's arms. The strains of the jingle hung in the air as they stayed in position, wearing grins of delighted anticipation. Even before Mr. Danziger stood up and came toward them, they knew they had a hit on their hands.

"Harris!" Mr. Danziger bounced over to the group, his hand outstretched. "What was the idea of all that other garbage? This is what I wanted. This is just what my soap should look like! You kids are great, by the way." He started with Walt and shook his hand forcefully, then went over to Pres and patted him on the back. "Did I tell you you were great?"

"You just did, sir." Mary Ellen smiled over at

Patrick, who had been taking pictures like crazy. At her glance, he put the camera down and blew her a kiss.

"Harris," Mr. Danziger waggled a finger in the director's face, "it was a joke, right, that other thing? Why didn't you tell me you had this just the way I wanted it? It's perfect."

"Well, ah, actually. . . ." Harris looked over at Dan for some logical explanation, but since there was none, he simply sat there. "I wasn't sure which concept you would prefer. You see, we often come up with a splashy treatment and a solid treatment and let the client decide. Yes, that's it," he said, warming to his lie. "We let the client decide. Glad you like it, Mr. Danziger. Really glad."

"Thanks for a job well done." Mr. Danziger straightened his tie as he walked toward the door. "I know now that the national spot for Clean Soap will *look* clean and *be* clean. That's the key to my life, you know. Clean living. You kids are great," he murmured as he left the room.

The door shut with a clang behind him. Suddenly, everyone was talking at once.

"We did it!" Walt hugged Olivia so hard, she yelled.

"Tarenton wins again!" Pres swung Mary Ellen and Angie around in a circle.

"But what about me?" Vanessa ran over to her mother in despair. Mrs. Barlow tried to soothe her little girl's ruffled feathers, but Vanessa wasn't having any of it. "I'll get back at them somehow for cutting my hair," she growled. "Can't we sue, Mom?"

"Kids, why didn't you tell me what you had in mind?" Harris was flustered, but happy.

"Maybe because you wouldn't have listened to them, Mr. Scheckner," Ardith pointed out. She was so proud of her group, she could have kissed them all, except that they wouldn't have stood still for that kind of sentimentality.

"Listened? Naturally, I would have," Harris sputtered. "Dan and I are reasonable men. We know what's what."

"Well," Pres commented, folding his arms on his chest with a self-satisfied smile, "you didn't seem to appreciate us for our real qualities, Mr. Scheckner. I mean, you picked us for our squeaky clean look, right? And that's what your product needed. If we looked like that" — he pointed at Vanessa — "nobody would have believed a word of that soap jingle. You see, you may think we seem like hicks, but maybe we understand things you don't."

Harris pushed his dark glasses up on top of his head and nodded sagely, as though he had just heard the most brilliant comment ever uttered. "I have to hand it to you," he murmured. "Out of the mouths of babes," he quoted to Dan. "They're right! What more can I say? They're absolutely right."

"What about it, Mr. Scheckner? If they're going to be taping this routine tomorrow, they better get some rehearsal in," Ardith reminded the director. "They do look good, I'll agree, but they could be better."

The cheerleaders smiled at one another, acknowledging Ardith's statement. She never let them get away with anything, including perfection, if she thought it could be slightly more perfect. What would they have done without her?

"Let's take it from the top, then," Harris nodded. "Ah, Vanessa, would you get out of the way, dear? You're holding up the works."

With a whoop of laughter, the six cheerleaders assembled in place for the commercial. They waited for their cue, and then they threw themselves into the routine. The harder the moves, the easier they made them look. Today was their day, and no one could take it away from them.

CHAPTER

12

"You're sure you don't want to come celebrate with us, Pres?" Olivia asked. It was snowing outside, but that didn't matter to the cheerleaders.

"No, think I'll pass. I want to say good-bye to Blake," he told her quietly. "Since I'll probably never see her again," he added, feeling strange. It was one thing to have your real girl friend three thousand miles away in a hospital, but another to have made a friendship that was impossible to retain.

"Hey, that's not necessarily the case," Patrick reminded him. "You look like you have plenty of potential to be a jet-setter, man," he joked. But when he saw the expression on Pres's face, he didn't go on. He knew what it was to feel passionately about a girl. Except with Pres, it seemed to be two girls.

"Okay, well, we'll see you later, then," Mary Ellen said softly, picking up her coat. "Say thanks to Blake for us, will you?" She gently nudged

Patrick, who nodded and walked out of the hotel room, followed by Angie, Nancy, Walt, and Olivia. Mary Ellen closed the door behind them and stared at it for a minute before walking down the corridor to the elevators. Pres was an odd guy, no doubt about it. One minute you thought he ate nails for breakfast, and the next, he was moony-eyed over a girl he'd bumped into on the street.

Pres got up, went to the window, and looked at his watch. He was going to meet Blake in the Village at eight, and it was only seven now. He felt so antsy, like he was going to jump out of his skin. And when the phone rang, he literally did jump, his heart beating a rapid tattoo. What was he so nervous about, anyway?

"Hello?"

"Long distance for Preston Tilford. Is Mr. Tilford there?" an operator asked.

"Yeah, sure, go ahead. I mean, this is him. He." His heart was pounding now, because he knew who was on the other end of the line. Unless Claudia had already had the operation. Unless she was. . . .

"Pres? You there?" That silvery voice floated on the air currents to him.

"Claudia! I've been trying to get hold of you for days." He was so relieved, he could have cried. Only Pres didn't cry, ever.

"A likely story," she teased him. "Here I am, being poked and prodded and tested, and there you are, running around New York, living it up and having a wonderful time. I know 'cause I talked to your mama," she added.

"Claudia, stop tap-dancing and tell me how you are! What's going on?"

"So far, so good," she sighed. "They kept putting it off so they could fiddle around some more, but they've finally scheduled the operation for tomorrow. See, before they cut you open, they have to do all sorts of things. Blood tests, nerve tests, pins and needles everywhere. Oh, Pres!" She wanted to keep it light, but it was getting harder. She knew what was at stake here — and so did he.

"I wish I were with you, sweetheart. I wish I could just hold you through the whole thing."

"Me, too."

There was silence for a minute, and then Claudia took a deep breath. "I miss you so much, you know. It feels like you're a continent away. Well, you are," she laughed. "But it feels like you're so far away, I'll never see you again."

"Don't say that!" He practically yelled into the phone. Why had she repeated the very words he'd said about another girl just a few minutes ago? It was eerie. "It's going to work out fine. I feel it. I know you're going to sail right through this thing and recover in a couple of weeks."

"Six months is minimum, the doctors tell me," she said glumly. "You know, it's so dumb. I've felt fine as long as I can remember, and now they're making me put my life on the line." There was a little shake in her voice as she went on. "I can't help thinking that if I just went on the way I was — "

"You can't do that," Pres interrupted. "You know how dangerous that would be. I love you.

All I want is for you to get well and stay that way."

"Okay!" She suddenly shifted to high gear, forcing a laugh into her voice. "I guess, if you put it that way, I have absolutely no choice, then, have I? Got to get well so I can come home and squeeze the living daylights out of you. Get ready, mister," she threatened, "because I am going to rassle you to the ground like I was a big grizzly and you were some itty bitty raccoon." Her southern accent, which faded in and out depending on her mood, had become very pronounced. He could tell she was putting it on for his benefit. How he wished she would just let down all her defenses and be vulnerable, the way she'd been when they last saw each other. But maybe now there was too much at stake.

"You're going to have to try pretty hard, then. I'm strong as an ox now that I've been rehearsing round the clock." He wouldn't pity her; he knew how much she hated that.

"Say, how *is* that commercial going, anyhow?" she asked. "You going to be famous by the time I'm out of this chicken coop?"

"I certainly hope so."

And then, there was silence again. This time, neither of them could think of a thing to say.

"So, I guess I better let you get some rest, right? What time are they doing this thing?" Pres finally asked her.

"Bright and early. Just about seven, the doctor said."

"I'll be thinking about you. Thinking real hard."

"You better. When are you going back to Tarenton?"

"Tomorrow, after we do the final shoot. Should be home before dinner."

"Good. Soon as I wake up from the anesthesia, I'll call you with the results. Or have my mom give you a ring," she said lightly. The grim truth, as both of them well knew, was that someone else would have to call him if she wasn't able to.

"I love you, Claudia," he breathed gently. Then, "Good-night."

" 'Night, now."

Pres sat there for a minute beside the phone, feeling her in the room with him. As he raised his hand to rub his tired eyes, his watch came into view. "Oh, no! Blake!" he shouted. Grabbing his jacket, he was off and running down the hall. Then he remembered he hadn't locked the door, so he came back and did it, and sped to the elevator that was opening just as he returned.

By the time he arrived at the restaurant, a little burger joint below ground level way west on Bedford Street near the Hudson River, it was eight-thirty. Blake was leaning against the juke box up front, jamming quarters into the machine with frustrated intensity.

"I'm really sorry," Pres greeted her.

"There are such things as telephones, you know," she growled. "When someone is going to be late, it's customary in the civilized world to call and say so. Or don't you do that sort of thing in Tarenton?"

"Well, don't bite my head off." Pres threw up

his hands. "It was the traffic. And I had a phone call — long distance."

"I see." She was very tight and frosty. The waiter showed them to a booth and left them with menus. Blake opened hers and stared down into it. "I always swear I'm going to have something other than a burger here, and I never do."

"Well, live dangerously. Have the chili."

"Why should I?" It was a challenge. She looked across at him with piercing dark eyes that dared him to joke, dared him to so much as blink.

"Blake," he sighed, "I'm not really in a mood for sparring. What is it? Come clean."

"Nothing," she shrugged. "I'll have a burger and a Coke. What about you?"

"I'm going home tomorrow. Would that by any chance have anything to do with your foul mood?" he asked softly. Here he was, crazy in love with Claudia and yet he was going to miss Blake terribly. Was she just trying to make it easier for him to say good-bye with no regrets?

"Long-distance relationships are hard, man, real hard. Takes a better person than me." Blake tossed the words off as though she actually meant them.

"Blake, this is our last night together. Let's enjoy it, okay?" He took her hand, feeling her resistance. But his heart wasn't in it, because he was thinking about someone else, and she knew at once.

"Why don't you come clean with me, Preston? Why don't you just spit it out and say it. No, babe, I'm not gonna write, I'm not gonna call.

There's a little girl waiting for me back home in a red house with a white picket fence, and she's all I want. It was fun meeting you, but now it's over."

He had to laugh. "You still don't know a lot about me, do you? You still have some picture of me as the nice, clean-cut boy next door, right out of an old movie." He made a face. "Why don't you give me some credit for being a person, Blake — just like you?"

Her head shot up and she put her hand to her mouth, biting one nail furiously. "Okay, then tell me the real story. I can take it."

"There *is* someone else," he admitted. "I can't lie to you about her. And I can't pretend I'm not in love with her. Right now, she's in a hospital in California, and tomorrow they're going to operate on her, and it's really bad. . . ." His voice trailed off. "I should be with her. I shouldn't have even considered coming to New York to film a dumb commercial. I should have just gotten to California some way. What a selfish louse I am," he finished.

It was Blake's turn to take his hand, but he didn't pull away. "Hey, mister, go easy on yourself, will you?" She smiled gently. "Everybody has to live his own life, I guess. And whether you were with her or not, she'd still need to be strong on her own to come through the operation with flying colors. Isn't that right?"

Pres had to laugh. "You are the original tough guy, you know that, Blake? At least you think you are. Everybody has to do it on his own. Well, I guess I don't really believe in your philosophy. I think people have to help each other."

"Of course they do. I know that." She bit her lip, but she couldn't stop the tears. Two big glistening drops rolled down her smooth cheeks and landed on the table. She sniffed and wiped her eyes, and that was the end of her crying jag.

"Blake," Pres said after a minute, "have you ever been in love? Really in love?"

She thought about this, then shook her head. "Never let myself get involved. Never wanted my style cramped. Until now, that is," she added softly. "That girl in California better know how lucky she is."

Pres didn't tell her that he was praying and hoping that Claudia was blessed with luck. He could see the pain in Blake's eyes, and he suddenly understood how bad it could be, falling for a guy who didn't feel the same way. It was the first time in his life that he hadn't immediately put himself first, when he'd had perspective on somebody else's emotions. He felt her pain, and it hurt.

"Enough of this." Blake shook her head, as though she was trying to shake the bad thoughts out of it. "And now, for the fun part." She grinned, seemingly willing to start the evening all over again. "We are going to have such a wonderful time, you won't think about your troubles." The waiter brought their Cokes, and Blake lifted hers high in a toast. "To your girl friend — what's her name?"

"Claudia," Pres told her, savoring the sound of it. "Claudia Randall."

"To Claudia Randall. May she live to be a hundred."

"To Blake Norton," Pres countered. "One of the best things about New York."

The evening, from that point on, was a total success, and it remained light and comfortable until the moment when the taxi pulled up in front of Blake's house. Pres got out and waved the driver on, then stood with her on the pavement. In an instant, there were snowflakes in her dark hair, and in her lashes.

"This is good-bye then, Pres Tilford," Blake said, extending her hand. "It's been swell." She made a ridiculous face, then yanked her hand away, not looking at him as she ran for the door.

But Pres came after her. "I'm going to miss you," he said, putting a hand on her shoulder. "I really wish we had the time to get to know each other." He smiled, reaching over to touch a snowflake on her face. "I think we could be very good friends."

"Yeah, well, them's the breaks." She shrugged. Then she looked at him appraisingly. "Maybe someday, I'll come see your little Tarenton. Wouldn't you just fall down in a faint if I waltzed into town one day?"

"I'd like it." He pulled her to him, kissing her full lips gently. Then they both pulled away, until just their hands were touching. "Thanks for everything," he whispered.

"Thank you," she said simply. "It's not everyday you bump into a prince." And then she was off, like Cinderella escaping before the midnight hour caught up with her and turned all her good intentions into dust.

Pres watched her vanish through the door, then slowly walked down Eighty-sixth Street to the subway. He saw Blake's face, then Claudia's, then Blake's again. But in a minute, all he saw was the snow.

Mary Ellen and Patrick said good-night a few times. The first time was when the others left them in the hotel lobby, since they clearly wanted to be alone. They wandered around the quiet floor, holding hands, not even speaking, finally going to the big window to watch the traffic plowing down Seventh Avenue in the snow. The second time they said good-night was in the elevator on the way up to their floor. No one was around, so Patrick took the opportunity to unbutton Mary Ellen's coat and reach in to put his hands around her waist.

"So warm," he sighed, bending over to drop a tender kiss on the side of her neck.

"You, too." She smiled, linking her arms around his neck. Since the cheerleaders' great success that afternoon, she'd been in a perfectly wonderful mood, and she was more receptive to Patrick now than she'd been all week. She didn't know why, exactly, but she was looking forward to going home, to being in her own world again. And Patrick was an important part of that world.

The elevator doors opened, revealing the empty corridor. "Where's everybody?" Mary Ellen murmured.

"Who cares?" Patrick didn't want to let her

go — not now. "Pres is probably still out, and I bet Walt is in your room, sharing the highlights of the day. Which means. . . ."

"Which means your room is probably vacant, right?" Mary Ellen smiled.

"We could look and find out." He'd never felt that she was so accessible, so open to him. It wasn't that he wanted to take advantage of the situation. He would have been perfectly happy just holding her all night long.

"I have to be brilliant in the morning, Patrick," Mary Ellen said with as much sincerity as she could muster. She really did want to stay with him, more now than she ever had. What had changed her mind? Was it the craziness of New York, the chaos of the past week?

"You're brilliant, anyway," he told her, stroking the luxurious golden hair away from her forehead. "But I get the message. It's good-night." He kissed the tips of her fingers and wrenched himself away.

"Patrick?" She stood in front of her door, fingering the key in her pocket. "Thank you for standing by me this week. I don't know how I would have managed it if you hadn't been there."

He grinned, but stayed where he was. "So, what's the verdict? Are you still coming back here to take New York by storm some day?"

Actually, she had made a personal vow that this wouldn't be the end of it. How could she say she had really given the chase a fair chance? Maybe she just wasn't ready for New York — or New York wasn't ready for her.

"Some day, maybe. Not now, though." Despite

the awe and love she bore for this wonderful city, she wanted something softer, something easier. She wanted to be a star cheerleader, and to have her friends around her, and to have the guy who was nuts about her continue to be so.

They smiled at one another, a look of understanding passing between them. They had forged a bond together, and it was a powerful one. It was strong enough to withstand hurts and deceptions, even to withstand Mary Ellen's ambition. But was it stronger than that? Patrick shook his head and opened the door of his hotel room. Mary Ellen did the same. And without a word, they walked inside and closed their separate doors.

CHAPTER

13

"**A**re you sure you have everything?" Nancy was rifling through drawers and closets, absolutely certain that they were going to leave something vital in New York.

"Positive." Angie grinned. She was seated on the bed, filing her nails. "Will you calm down, please?"

"They say if you leave something behind in a place you're visiting, it means you unconsciously want to return there," Mary Ellen told the others. "Maybe I should *consciously* forget something."

"You'll be back," Olivia nodded, tying her hair back in a no-nonsense ponytail. "I can guarantee it."

The door opened and Ardith flew in, the freshly pressed Tarenton uniforms over her arm. "Are you people ready to check out? Because we hardly have time for breakfast, let alone a warm-up. And Harris said we should be at the studio early enough for makeup and last minute notes before the final taping."

"We've been ready for an hour," Angie informed her.

"Good, fine. Listen, here's my key — I'm going on ahead to the studio. Harris took care of the bill, so you guys check out and meet me there." She was out the door before the girls could object.

Mary Ellen slung her coat over her arm, picked up her suitcase and the duffle that held her practice equipment, and started for the door. "Goodbye, room," she said softly. "I had a wonderful time."

Nancy chuckled at her friend's intensity, but she had to admit that she, too, had been changed by New York City. There was an excitement to everyday life here that you just didn't feel in Tarenton. It was hard to say whether this was because it was New York or because it was just a new place where everyday life held a variety of unexpected events. But as she stacked her bags by the door, she, too, hoped silently that she would come back some day.

Angie and Olivia were more matter-of-fact about their departure. Neither girl had really been infatuated with the big city, and although they'd had fun, they were itching to get home.

"Except how are we going to tell them we didn't bring back one single souvenir?" Angie moaned, as Mary Ellen pressed the elevator button.

"That is awful," Olivia agreed. "Not even an I-Love-New-York T-shirt or anything. And how are we going to explain that we lost all their money?" She looked up as she saw the boys closing the door of their room. "Oh, good, they didn't oversleep," she grinned as Walt walked toward her, loaded with luggage.

"Are you by any chance accusing us?" he growled, bending over to give her a hearty good morning kiss.

"I want some departure shots," Patrick insisted, aiming the camera at the group. The cheerleaders obliged by assuming ridiculous positions around the bags: Angie and Pres got down on their hands and knees, Olivia climbed on top of them, and Mary Ellen, Nancy, and Walt sprawled happily on the floor. They were all laughing over how silly they looked when the Barlows' door opened and Vanessa and her mother walked out. They both paused for a minute, staring at the laughing crew, and then they walked solemnly down the hall toward the other elevator bank.

As Vanessa passed them, she looked down with an expression on her face that would have shattered glass. "Don't you have any sense of decency?" she said. "Suppose some other hotel guests came out of their rooms and saw you like this."

"Well, then, I guess they'd think we were just dopey out-of-towners who were having a super-terrific time," Walt shrugged.

"They'd think we all really liked each other," Olivia continued, scrambling to her feet. "Which we do." The elevator in their bank arrived and the door slowly eased its way open.

Vanessa shook her head the way she always

used to when it had lots of thick, dark hair on it, and then she realized she wasn't getting the same effect out of her shorn locks. She stalked past the group and waited with her mother until the elevator came. She looked very, very annoyed.

"Somehow, I don't think this trip will hold happy memories for her." Walt shrugged, holding the elevator door so the others could pile their luggage inside.

The lobby was jammed with a convention just coming in and a busload of Japanese tourists going out. Mary Ellen took everybody's keys and fought her way forward to stand in the checkout line as the others got out of the way of traffic and waited on the other side of the lobby.

"Yes? May I help you?" A short young man wearing a badly cut brown suit smiled at her briefly as he took the keys.

"These are for Rooms 413, 417, and 420," she said, looking up at the magnificent chandeliers above her head. No doubt about it, she was going to miss this place.

"Of course. If you'll wait just a moment." The man turned to his files.

"Oh, we're all paid for and everything," she told him, turning away.

"Just a minute, please." The man flipped through his books, then looked up at her with a blank expression on his face. "You've occupied these rooms since Thursday, is that correct?"

"Yes," she said, nodding.

"This is for the Tarenton group? Mrs. Engborg — is that the name?"

"That's right."

"And you say the rooms have been paid for? I have no record here of — "

"But Mrs. Engborg said. . . ." Mary Ellen looked puzzled. "Could you look under Harris Scheckner's name?" she asked. "He was supposed to have taken care of the bill for us."

The clerk frowned, flipping through his files. "Nothing under a Harris Scheckner, no. I'm going to have to ask you for payment in full, miss, and immediately. Otherwise. . . ." He didn't finish his sentence, but gave her a menacing scowl that clearly said he meant business.

Mary Ellen looked around in a panic. "There must be some mistake." She waved urgently at the group and they started right over.

"I assure you, there's no mistake, miss," the clerk said, very angry now. "You owe us for three double rooms for six nights at $85 per room per night, which makes. . . ." He totaled the amount quickly on his adding machine. "That's a total of $1,530, plus your taxes and surcharge for the extra beds in two of the rooms. You had breakfast here each morning, and dinner for some of your party on two nights. That's an additional $315.27, minus your two-hundred-dollar deposit."

"Oh, no," Mary Ellen moaned, dropping her head into her hands. "Oh, please say this isn't so! We don't have any money."

"It is most certainly so, miss," the young man said, his small eyes regarding her with contempt. "I'm afraid I'd better get the manager." He stalked off to the back room, his heels clicking on the marble floor.

"What is it?" Pres asked, seeing the anxious look on Mary Ellen's face. "You look like you just got arrested."

She gulped and bit her lower lip. "This is nothing to joke about, Pres. We're in trouble."

"What are you talking about?" Nancy demanded.

The manager approached the desk with the young clerk, and he wasn't even trying to look pleasant. He started in on them right away. "You kids think you came to town for a free ride? Well, I'd suggest you think again. Refusal to pay a bill, no matter the size of it, is a very serious offense. And yours," he tapped a finger on the paper in front of him, "is quite an extensive bill."

"But why would Harris have said he'd take care of things if he didn't intend to?" Angie moaned.

"Young lady," the manager said, glaring at Angie. "I'm a very busy person. You'll have to come up with full payment, or I'm going to have to let the police handle it."

"Oh, boy." Walt looked at the ceiling. "Last night, the Plaza; tonight, Sing-Sing. How the mighty have fallen."

"Walt!" Olivia gave him a shove. "Oh, Melon, what are we going to do?"

"Quick, somebody get Harris on the phone. Tell him, unless he sends somebody over here with a check or a credit card, we're never going to make it to the shoot." Mary Ellen grimaced and went to the comfort of Patrick's arms. "I thought they just made you wash some dishes if you couldn't pay for what you ate in a restaurant. Looks like it's different with a hotel bill."

"Dishes? We'd be lucky if they made us scrub the entire building." Patrick looked rather grim.

"I'll call," Angie offered. "Somebody give me a dime."

"Phone calls in New York cost a quarter," the manager growled. "And the rest of you, stay right here where I can see you."

Pres handed Angie a quarter and proceeded to sink into the nearest chair. Nancy and Walt stood nervously by the desk with Mary Ellen, and Olivia and Patrick started pacing. They were each trying to come up with some brilliant scheme for keeping the manager from calling the police, but none of them was succeeding.

"You people still here?" A husky voice right above Pres's shoulder made them turn around. It was Vanessa, wrapped up in as much dignity as she could still muster. "Dan did say he wanted you early," she added. Then she noticed the somber mood of the group. "Is anything wrong?" There was a hopeful note in her voice.

"No, nothing," Walt hastened to assure her.

"Wait a minute. Mrs. Barlow could help us," Olivia reminded him, pointing over to the desk where Vanessa's mother was talking to the young clerk. "It's a slim one, but it's our only chance, Walt."

Then she turned to Vanessa with a reasonable smile on her face. "Van, actually, we *are* having a little problem. See, the trouble is that Harris promised he'd pay our hotel bill and he must have forgotten. We're sure he's going to give us a check the instant we get to the studio, but right now, the important thing is getting to the taping on time. Do you think your mother could just put this little extra amount on her credit card and Harris will pay her right back?"

Vanessa's eyes lit up. "You mean, you can't get out of here until you've paid your bill?"

"Right." Mary Ellen nodded. "It's really silly. Just a question of making the manager happy. Do you think your mom would — "

"Are you out of your mind?" Vanessa was grinning now. "Why should I help you? Here you've been so thrilled with yourselves throughout this whole trip, so spiteful because I got the lead in the commercial first, so happy when it didn't work out my way. And now, when it comes down to the crunch, you want me to help you? Only a bunch of idiots would believe that life could work out that way. You're getting exactly what you deserve." She started over toward her mother, and Walt dashed in front of her.

"Mrs. Barlow, please," he panted, "can I just have a second of your time?" The woman looked slightly puzzled, but she put down her bag and nodded.

"Mother, don't listen to him," Vanessa interjected quickly. "He has some dreadful plan about us paying everybody's bill. It's too embarrassing to discuss." And with that, she hustled her mother out the door, staying behind just long enough to give Walt a devastating sneer. "I wonder if Har-

151

ris might just change his mind about me, if I happened to get over to the studio right away. It's certainly worth a try." And then she walked away, the eagerness to do the cheerleaders one better written all over her face.

"Oh, I wish she'd fall down a manhole," Walt sighed. "Ange!" He raced back to the group just as Angie was returning from the phone bank. "What's going on?" he demanded.

Angie shook her head. "Not good. The receptionist said that Harris and Casey had to go meet Mr. Danziger someplace for a breakfast meeting, and she doesn't know where they are or what time they'll be back. I told her what had happened, and she said she'd tell Harris as soon as he called in. Then I talked to Ardith. She's on her way over, but there's not a whole lot she can do. Her credit card has an upper limit of $500. That's just a drop in our bucket."

"Oh, fine," Nancy breathed. "Pres, do you think you could get hold of Blake at her school? I know it's awful to impose on her any more, but maybe her father could bail us out temporarily."

Pres bit his lip. "I never asked her what school she went to. And who knows if she ever mentioned me to her folks."

Patrick's handsome face was creased with worry. "Money! Why is it always money? This is a terrific end to our great time in the city, right?" He punched one fist into the other palm and paced some more.

Mary Ellen came over to put a hand on his arm. "Well, maybe we weren't destined for

152

stardom. Maybe somebody's telling us something."

"I wouldn't care about losing out on the stardom," Olivia said nervously. "It's losing our freedom that really gets to me. Do you get a trial first, before they throw you in jail?"

There was suddenly a lot of noise and commotion in the lobby, and Patrick had to raise his voice to talk above it. "This town, I don't know . . ." he grumbled loudly.

"What's that?" Angie stood up abruptly, pointing at the front desk.

"What's what?" Mary Ellen asked glumly.

A small dark man wearing a squashed tweed wool cap was waving his hands wildly at the manager, trying to make himself understood, and the manager kept motioning him away. There was something about the man that made Angie pause, then smile.

"Do you remember the night we came into town? The taxidriver?" she said, narrowing her eyes to stare intently at the man making a fuss at the desk.

"Right," Walt agreed. "That's him."

The others looked around to see the cabdriver pounding on the desk, making a very big deal out of something or other. The manager was refusing to even listen to him. "Let's go over and say hi," Pres suggested. "Not much else we can do right now."

They arrived at the desk in time to hear the man yelling at the manager. "Mr. T. Ghali, that's my name. You can look at my Medallion — I'm parked right in front of your darn hotel."

153

"Look, mister, I'm not telling you anything about what tourists come in and out of here over the course of a week," the manager growled. "That's privileged information."

"But their money!" The little man was practically jumping up and down now. "I have all their money, don't you understand, you turkey?"

"What did you say?" Angie was by his side immediately, tugging on his sleeve. "Please, did you say you'd found some money in your cab?"

"Yes, of course," Mr. Ghali nodded vehemently. "But I'm not saying how much or where it was until I know I've got the right — " He stopped, then opened his eyes wider, taking her in. "You, were you with some other kids?" he asked.

"It's us! We're with her," Nancy told him adamantly, pointing out her companions. "Do you remember? You drove us in from LaGuardia last Thursday?"

"And what were you coming to New York to do?" he asked, demanding the right answer before he'd cough up the cash.

"To film a soap commercial," Pres reminded him. "We had you sing it with us."

"Aha!" Mr. Ghali smiled triumphantly at the hotel manager. "Finally, the right hotel! I've been driving around this city since Thursday, trying to remember where I dropped you folks off. Not that many people want to stay at *this* hotel," he muttered to the manager.

"Well, I'm glad that's settled," the manager huffed. "These kids claimed they couldn't pay their hotel bill. So now, if you'd just hand over what you found so that they can count it — "

"Not on your life!" Mr. Ghali folded his arms over his chest. "I want to hear that jingle first. Just to make sure I've got the right bunch. This is a lot of money, and I want to be certain it doesn't fall into the wrong hands."

Walt looked at the others and they all grinned. "We'll sing it for you, mister. Positions, kids!" He moved a few stray tourists out of the way.

The cheerleaders and Patrick lined up and took off. "Clean, Clean is bubble; Clean, Clean is pure," they began, dancing a path right through the people who had gathered around to watch. By the time they'd come to the end of the song, the entire lobby full of tourists and staff were smiling and clapping. They finished with a flourish, and then Angie got up out of her split and went over to Mr. Ghali.

"Now do you believe us?" she asked.

"I believe you," he said.

Just then, the hotel doors burst open and Harris ran in, breathless, with Ardith and Casey right behind him. Mr. Danziger was right on their heels, panting and clutching his hat.

"How could I be so stupid as to waltz out of the studio without giving you guys a check?" Harris smacked the heel of his hand against his forehead. "Casey, how could you let me get away with something like that?" He stuck his watch in her face. "We're late as it is. Now will you please settle their bill so we can get moving? Mr. Danziger is anxious to see the final product."

"It's okay, Mr. Scheckner," Walt grinned. "We've found our money. This man was about to give it back to us."

"Yes?" Harris looked at Mr. Ghali, who had a very determined expression on his face. He wasn't giving up anything. "Well, let's do it. Just give the stuff back, mister. Do you read me loud and clear? We don't want trouble."

Mr. Ghali handed the makeup case to Angie, ignoring Harris. "Been singing your jingle to myself ever since you got out of my cab. Tell you what, kids. When you get through with work today, I'm taking you back to LaGuardia. My treat."

"That's, ah, that's really great." Pres laughed. "Thanks. We could use a free ride."

"Well?" Ardith put her hands on her hips, looking at her incorrigible group with a great deal of affection and admiration. "You kids get going. Casey and I will take care of things here." She put out her hand, and Angie gratefully put the makeup case into it.

"From now on, this is in your custody. As a matter of fact, I may let you keep it permanently," she told her coach.

Mr. Danziger cleared his throat and started for the door. "Can we get these kids out of here and to work, Harris?" he asked. "We've got a commercial to film."

"We're ready as we'll ever be, Mr. Danziger." Mary Ellen grinned, walking away from the hotel manager with a look of confidence on her face.

156

CHAPTER

Pres crawled into bed as soon as he got home, but he had no intention of going to sleep. He was exhausted from too many hours in airports — they'd had to change planes in Chicago and there'd been a delay because of a heavy snowfall — but he didn't think he'd be able to close his eyes until he knew something — anything. Whether it was good news or bad.

He punched the area code and number, then waited. It was seven P.M. in California. The switchboard answered and he gave the number of Claudia's room. Then he waited. The phone rang three times, four times, eight times. Nobody picked up.

"Darn!" He jumped out of bed, digging his heels into the plush beige carpet. There was an ache in his gut that matched the one in his heart. Where was she now? What were they doing to her? In New York, everything had seemed so distant, so unreal. But now, back home in his own room, it was hard to deny the fact that the outcome of Claudia's life had already been decided, and he had no idea what it was. It made him feel so alone, so helpless.

He tried again a half hour later, and then an hour after that. And still, no answer. He dialed again and demanded of the lady at the switchboard that he speak to somebody in charge, but none of the nurses he managed to get on the phone would give him any information. He paced his room again, looking out at the bright stars that shone in through his window. Then he threw himself back onto the bed, anxious and upset. The night passed; he lay there tossing and turning, finally falling into an uneasy sleep by dawn.

He went to school late and wandered around in a daze. His classmates were dying for the scoop on New York, and his fellow cheerleaders were having a great time describing their adventures, but he couldn't get into any of it.

"Meet us at the mall at four, okay?" He was standing in the hallway between classes, staring into space, when Mary Ellen's voice penetrated his fog. "We're going to air the tape Harris gave us in front of Marnie's on Mrs. Gunderson's video machine. Practically everyone in school's coming."

"What? Oh, yeah, if I can make it. Maybe I'll see you later." He saw the confused look on her face, but he didn't feel that he owed her any explanations. He was close to Melon and yet he was too wrapped up in his concerns to want to share them. This was just something he'd have to deal with by himself.

He got into his Porsche as soon as his last class was over and revved the engine. It always made him feel better to go for a drive, fast, speeding along the outskirts of the lake. Today, it didn't work. He pushed the machine, got it to behave just the way he liked it to, made it race and plummet down hills and across open spaces, but he still felt lousy. He turned the car around and started for home.

Nobody was around, so he went to his room and lay down on the bed. He'd never felt so miserable, so filled with a sense of dread. He looked at the phone, wanting to try again but afraid of getting an answer. He'd gone so long without knowing now, that it seemed he never would. He'd have to walk around in this fog for the rest of his life.

The phone rang, and he jumped before reaching for it. Probably one of the kids wanting to find out why he hadn't showed up at the mall yet. They all wanted to yammer about the wonderful week in New York. Maybe he should let it ring and they'd go away. But it was probably just easier to say hi and tell them he was expecting a call so he couldn't talk. He picked up on the fourth ring.

"Pres? Is this Pres?" It was a soft female voice he didn't recognize.

"Yeah. Who's calling?"

"I'm Mrs. Randall. Claudia's mother."

His heart almost stopped beating. He was inarticulate in the face of what this woman might have to tell him, and he could feel his tongue sticking to the roof of his mouth. "How is she?" he finally gasped through tightly clenched teeth. "What happened?"

"She's wonderful," her mother said, breaking down. Sobs wracked her, and she couldn't go on. "Here, I'll let her tell you herself."

There was a pause, and then Claudia came on the line. She sounded fuzzy and hesitant. "Pres? I'm fine. I came through with flying colors. They said it was touch and go for a while, but since I'm a fighter, they were never that worried. I'm going to be okay," she repeated, almost as though she didn't quite believe it. "I'm going to walk, and swim and . . . and boogie!"

Pres felt the tears coming — he couldn't stop them. "Oh, God, I'm so . . . Claudia, I never knew I could want anything so much as for you to get through this. I miss you so much. I was panicky when I couldn't get in touch with you. I've been calling and calling."

"I was kind of in and out of the anesthesia all day, or I would have picked up the phone. Sorry I made you worry." She sighed happily, and that one sound told him, more than anything, how glad she was to be alive.

"I wish I could be with you," he whispered.

"Me, too. In time, Pres. I have to stick around here for a while, but I'll be back in Tarenton before you can turn around." She was quiet for a minute, and then she whispered, "I'm really sleepy. Had a rough day and a half, if you know what I mean. Why don't you call tomorrow after school?"

"Done," he agreed.

"Hey," she asked. "You know why I made it? Because I told those doctors my boyfriend was going to be in a commercial on national TV, and I had to be there to watch it with him."

"I'm going over to see it right now. And to tell everybody that you're well."

"Do that. And Pres?"

"Yes?"

"I love you." She hung up quickly, slightly embarrassed at her long-distance confession. It was okay, though, she thought, as she sank back into sleep. Everything was okay.

Pres was in his car and on the road, singing, within minutes. Incredible how things had all turned around in such a quick period of time. He was in love with life, in love with the other drivers on the road, in love with the world. And he couldn't wait to shout his good news to everyone he knew.

"Oh, I wish you could have been there!" Nancy led Ben down the aisles of Pineland Mall. She'd been talking nonstop ever since she got home. "It was fun, but it would have been more fun to share it with you."

"I have to kiss you — now, this second," he insisted. "I've been going stir-crazy every night without you."

"I'll bet," she said indignantly, secretly pleased because he was probably serious. Ben had floated

161

from girl to girl before Nancy, but now, he was as faithful as could be.

"Seriously, though. . . ." Ben let the words trail off as he drew Nancy under the cover of a potted palm. His arms were tight around her, nearly squeezing the breath out of her.

"Hey, wait!" She laughed, slightly embarrassed because they were in such a busy place.

"No more waiting," Ben said, firmly planting his lips on hers. He felt her relax in his arms, giving in willingly to his embrace. "I needed that. A week without you is impossible!" He reached for her again, and she giggled. He was incorrigible.

"Ben, we have plenty of time for this. The tape! I really want you to see it — and they won't start till we show up."

"But there's something more important I have to do right now," he exclaimed urgently.

"What?"

"That terrific spot right below your left ear . . . I have to kiss it." He tried, but she wasn't buying.

"Later," she said stolidly, and dragged him off to Marnie's.

The others were all impatient to see the results of their adventure in New York. Walt was working the tape machine as Olivia poked and prodded him to get going and Ardith looked on in amused silence. Mary Ellen and Patrick were busy showing a gaping group of kids all of Patrick's still shots of New York, which he'd hurriedly developed in the school darkroom. Angie was regaling Mrs. Gunderson with the tale of how her makeup case was lost and found, meanwhile clutching her purse under her arm as though she was certain it was going to run away from her if she wasn't careful.

"Was it really the best city in the world?" Shelley Eismar demanded.

"I bet you miss it already," Susan Yardley sighed enviously.

"Yeah, kinda." Walt grinned. "But it's sort of nice to be home."

"I know I'd be crazy about New York," Chuck Maxwell, a star player on the Tarenton basketball team, said. "All those tall buildings — I'd really identify." He nodded, pulling himself up to his full six feet four.

"Here we are! We can start!" Nancy propelled a rather reluctant Ben over to the assembled group. More kids had joined them. There were about fifty of them now, all clamoring to see the rough print of the Clean Soap commercial, which Harris had given the cheerleaders as a going-away present.

"Not yet," Mary Ellen said softly. "Let's wait awhile for Pres. He said he'd try to get here."

"Where is he?" Angie asked.

Mary Ellen shook her head. "Claudia," she reminded her friend. That was all she had to say.

As they were standing around, they heard a peal of husky laughter. "No, silly, be careful! I can't go that fast!" It was Vanessa, wearing a maroon and black jogging outfit and hobbling along on crutches. She was being ably supported by one of Tarenton's largest football players, a beefy halfback named Jim Taylor.

Olivia looked toward them and made a face.

163

"Who invited her?" she grumbled. "And what's she doing on crutches?"

"She generally invites herself," Walt said, shrugging. "Hey, who cares? She can't spoil this." He pushed the rewind button and the tape machine whirred obediently. By the time it was back at zero and ready to play, however, Vanessa was right beside them. She was holding onto Jim for dear life, dangling her bandaged right foot in the air.

"What are you up to, boys and girls?" she asked sarcastically. "Are you all proud of your little effort? Going to show off to the crowd?" She turned to the people nearest her. "What they didn't tell you, I'm sure, was that everything was completely different back in New York. They were just the background dancers and I was the solo performer. If I hadn't tripped over that ridiculous curb outside the hotel and sprained my ankle, you'd be watching me up there."

"Sure, Vanessa." Chuck Maxwell was laughing so hard it was difficult for him to speak. "And next week you're starring in a Hollywood movie. It's called *The Invasion of the Punk Cuts*."

"Well, I *could* be in a movie," she said huffily. "I don't know why you don't believe me." There was a particularly nasty expression on her face. She hated the fact that everyone agreed her hair was perfectly awful.

"Because there's nothing wrong with your leg," Susan Yardley told her pointedly. "I saw you coming out of the bathroom early this morning when you thought no one was looking. You were walking just fine — on the bandaged foot, too."

Vanessa's face turned white with rage. "I was just testing it," she growled.

"*Sure* you were. Vanessa," Olivia suggested. "Why don't you take a walk. Or else sit still and watch our tape with everyone else."

"I'd rather go shopping," she spat out. And with that, she thrust her crutches at the boy she'd come in with and stalked off, her plans for gaining sympathy completely foiled.

Pres, hurrying toward Marnie's, nearly had a head-on collision with the furious Vanessa. "Hey, what'd you do to her?"

"We ruined her day," Mary Ellen said, smiling delightedly. She looked at him anxiously. "Well . . ." she ventured, "how are you?"

"I am *wonderful*. Super. Never been better." Pres jumped in the air and kicked his heels together. "I just spoke to Claudia and she's great. Life is wonderful," he added, grabbing Angie and Mary Ellen around the waist and giving them each a hug.

Patrick slapped him on the back; Walt came over to shake his hand. There were shouts of congratulations from the crowd, and Pres acknowledged them all. When things had settled down again, Chuck Maxwell grinned and pointed to the tape machine. "How about it, guys? We came for a show, you know."

Walt pushed the play button, and the Clean Soap jingle blasted through the speakers. On the screen, six very enthusiastic, totally committed cheerleaders danced and sang their hearts out, giving their all for Tarenton and for the product they represented.

Mary Ellen looked at herself on screen, then stole a glance at Patrick's proud face. She was back on home territory now, back where she belonged. And yet, she would never be the same. Whatever her future held in store, this trip to New York had in some mysterious way molded and shaped it. It wasn't a question of whether she would go back, she felt certain. It was when.

Angie watched the proceedings with a self-satisfied smile on her face. She looked good up there, better than she'd imagined. Sometimes she had a real inferiority complex — but it clearly was unfounded. She was a team player, and that was something to be proud of. Even if she had lost all their money, it was back safe and sound.

Walt and Olivia had their arms around each other as they watched, and weren't paying much attention to the tape. It was great to be back in Tarenton again, great to be able to have gone off and succeeded at what they so desperately desired to accomplish. Olivia knew her mother would have something to complain about when she saw the commercial, but that didn't matter. And Walt knew that his parents, rooted in the world of show business as they were, wouldn't be terribly impressed by his accomplishment. But that was okay, because he had Olivia.

Nancy watched herself perform with just a touch of regret. It had been scary in the big city, but exciting, too. Now that she'd seen herself in that other setting, it might be hard to accept what life in Tarenton had to offer. It was safe here, and it was nice to have Ben so attentive and affectionate, but that wasn't all there would be to her life, was it? She hoped for something more, though she didn't know what.

Only Pres could watch with total detachment. He saw himself on the screen, and it was as if someone else was up there — that guy who'd been in New York, while the real Pres had been miles away with the girl he loved. He thought briefly about Blake, and wondered whether she was doing okay. Then he thought about Claudia, and the picture of her beautiful face took his total and complete attention. He hoped it always would.

"That was great! Incredible!" Chuck Maxwell was clearly impressed.

"Let's see it again. But live this time," Susan Yardley suggested.

"Well. . . ." Angie was suddenly overwhelmed with all these people. Their classmates weren't the only ones in the mall. About a hundred passersby had stopped to watch the show.

"Go on," Shelley Eismar encouraged her. "It's just like doing it at a game."

So the six cheerleaders, grinning like Cheshire cats, lined up in position on the runway in front of Marnie's. Mary Ellen gave the nod and they were off, recreating the famous moment that everyone had just seen on film.

> "Wash your face,
> Wash it with Clean.
> Your skin will be the best,
> That it's ever been.
> Make it Clean . . .
> Get it Clean . . .
> You'll be Clean!"

The girls double back-flipped into somersaults, and Pres and Walt were waiting to catch them. They lifted Nancy and Angie on their shoulders, and Olivia sprang up onto Mary Ellen's. The six of them were flying now, back in the swing of everyday life and glad to be here. The trip had been wonderful, the glory delicious; but there was something nice about reaping their rewards back on home turf. Living it up in New York was a fairy tale come true, and it had given them all a boost they really needed, but what they needed more was what they had right now: the friendship, the teamwork, and the sheer joy that came from being the Tarenton cheerleaders.

There was a special glow on all their faces as they came to the final line of the song and joined hands, laughing. Being away had only made them more conscious of what they had here. If they were lucky, they would keep this spirit of togetherness for a long time to come, regardless of whatever new problems challenged them in the future. They owed it all — the tough parts as well as the easy ones — to one another.

When tragedy strikes one of the cheerleaders, the whole squad is affected. Read Cheerleaders #15, WAITING.

Books chosen with you in mind from

—Pass the word.

Living...loving...growing.
That's what **POINT** books are all about!
They're books you'll love reading and
will want to tell your friends about.

Don't miss these other exciting **Point** titles!

NEW POINT TITLES! $2.25 each

☐ QI 33306-2 **The Karate Kid** B.B. Hiller
☐ QI 31987-6 **When We First Met** Norma Fox Mazer
☐ QI 32512-4 **Just the Two of Us** Hila Colman
☐ QI 32338-5 **If This Is Love, I'll Take Spaghetti** Ellen Conford
☐ QI 32728-3 **Hello...Wrong Number** Marilyn Sachs
☐ QI 33216-3 **Love Always, Blue** Mary Pope Osborne
☐ QI 33116-7 **The Ghosts of Departure Point** Eve Bunting
☐ QI 33195-7 **How Do You Lose Those Ninth Grade Blues?** Barthe DeClements
☐ QI 33550-2 **Charles in Charge** Elizabeth Faucher
☐ QI 32306-7 **Take It Easy** Steven Kroll
☐ QI 33409-3 **Slumber Party** Christopher Pike